# Pemberley
## Mistletoe

This book is a work of fan-fiction. Names, characters, dialogues, places and incidents are the products of a combination of Jane Austen's and the author's imagination or are used fictitiously. Any resemblance to actual events, locales, or persons, living or dead, is entirely coincidental.

Copyright ©2013 by Ayr Bray (Emmaline Hoffmeister)

Revised 2017 by Ayr Bray (Emmaline Hoffmeister)

Republication 2021 by Emmaline Hoffmeister

Edited by R.D. Brown

All rights reserved.

No part of this book may be reproduced, scanned, or distributed in any printed or electronic form without permission. Please do not participate in or encourage piracy of copyrighted materials in violation of the author's rights. Purchase only authorized editions.

Emmaline Hoffmeister Website http://www.emmalinehoffmeister.com.

"As an only child I often dreamed of a Christmas with lots of family around. Emmaline Hoffmeister delivers a story that perfectly satisfies those desires. *Pemberley Mistletoe* provides all the joy, pleasure, chaos, and angst that one would expect from a holiday party of nineteen."


"A continuing story formed with all the characters we loved and despised from *Pride and Prejudice*, you will not be disappointed."


"Christmas generally means presents, family, love in colors of red and green, kisses under the mistletoe, and drama; because what is family without some drama? Everyone is sure to love Emmaline Hoffmeister's latest novel when Pemberley is overrun with family just weeks after Darcy and Elizabeth marry."


"I really loved reading about Lizzy and Darcy's first Christmas together. *Pemberley Mistletoe* is a novel packed with not only drama and angst, but a tender love story. *Pemberley Mistletoe* is is my favorite novel that Emmaline Hoffmeister has written."

# Dedication

Love Eternal ... Eternal Love

Christmas generally means presents, family, love in colors of red and green, kisses under the mistletoe, and drama; because what is family without some drama?

# Pemberley Mistletoe

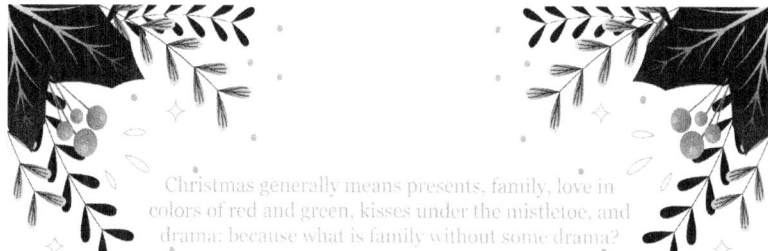

*a Novel by*

# EMMALINE HOFFMEISTER

## A PRIDE AND PREJUDICE SEQUEL

Original Author Name Ayr Bray

# Chapter 1

Fitzwilliam and Elizabeth Darcy had enjoyed a fortnight of being totally irresponsible with regard to anything other than matters of the heart. They had spent the first sennight of their marriage in London at the Darcys' townhouse. Although they left their residence rarely, they had the pleasure of enjoying an intimate family dinner with the Gardiners and some shopping on Bond Street for the Christmas season before they retired to the comforts of Pemberley, their family estate in the northern county of Derbyshire.

Since their arrival in Derbyshire, another sennight had passed. The servants were beginning to wonder if the master and his lovely new bride would ever emerge from their honeymoon chamber. Only the most trusted servants were allowed in, and then only to provide nourishment and draw the couple's bath. The closest anyone else was allowed was the chamber door.

The newlyweds' first venture from their room was nothing more than a walk to the Orangery. Elizabeth clung to the arm of her new husband while they walked, their heads bowed close together, sharing intimate secrets with whispered breaths.

Last summer, when Elizabeth had toured Pemberley with her Aunt and Uncle Gardiner, Mrs. Reynolds, the housekeeper, had praised the late Lady Anne Darcy's appreciation of the place. She had explained that Lady Anne had regularly conducted her guests on tours of the Orangery where they were known to admire not only the fruits within but the architecture without; its Italian design blended well with the style of Pemberley. Lady Anne had overseen the addition of two fountains and a grotto during her life, and had often entertained in the Orangery in the event the unpredictable northern England weather turned foul. Elizabeth had been well pleased with the place. Now, as mistress of the manor, it was even pleasanter than she imagined. The Orangery could be achieved by a passage from the west wing of the manor; thus one seeking the place need not leave the house. It was perfectly situated, and a relief against the all-too-frequently inclement winter weather Elizabeth was still becoming familiar with. The weather in Hertfordshire was certainly more temperate than the wild and untamed climes of the north.

Each day thereafter, the couple walked the halls of the manor and Elizabeth gradually became comfortable in her surroundings. She developed a genuine love and appreciation of the place and even had the opportunity to meet a few of the staff, though most were advised by Mrs. Reynolds to keep their distance until the master and mistress were ready to resume their daily responsibilities. Mrs. Reynolds anticipated it would be soon, for it was only one week before Miss Darcy, Colonel Fitzwilliam, and the Bingleys were to arrive.

"Fitzwilliam," Elizabeth said one morning before rising, "as much as I adore spending my days, and nights, here with you, I think we must emerge into the world. I have much to do, and little time to do it in."

"Alas, you are probably right, my dear," Fitzwilliam responded. "Mr. Carson has informed me twice that my steward is eager to discuss some small matters related to the modification of my investments now that I am married."

"I hope all is well. I would hate to learn that taking on a wife has burdened your finances." Elizabeth gave him a cheeky grin. "It would distress me greatly."

"What a little tease you are." Fitzwilliam reached for Elizabeth and drew her near, placing a tender kiss upon her lips. She accepted his sweet ministrations with pleasure.

"Come, let us face the world. Do not forget your sister and cousin are to arrive Friday, and Jane and Charles the day after. For my part, I must admit that I am excited to have them join us for our first Christmas together. I know we shall be a merry party." She looked towards her husband and girlishly giggled. "I think this will be my favourite Christmas ever, my first in my new home," she looked a little guilty as she leaned towards him and whispered, "and without my mother."

Elizabeth swung her legs over the side of the bed and energetically stood up to face the day. Her chestnut braid bounced against her back as she swung open the armoire doors to choose a gown. Turning her head to glance over her shoulder at her handsome husband, still lying in bed, she caught sight of him watching her. Pursing her lips, she blew him a kiss, flashed a saucy smile, and reached for her pale pink gown. Walking across the room, Elizabeth sat at her vanity and picked up her brush. "Fitzwilliam, be a dear and ring the bell for me. I would like Gracie to come help me with my hair."

Once Fitzwilliam rang the bell, he had no other choice; he must rise or be caught in Elizabeth's bed when the maid arrived. He had just finished putting on his robe and slippers when Gracie arrived using the servants' door.

Fitzwilliam had sent a message through Mr. Carson, his valet, to his steward informing him he was available to meet today. At the desired time, the man arrived with a satchel of documents in tow. Elizabeth had been sitting with Fitzwilliam in his study, occupying more of his attention than allowed him time to look over estate matters. A few months ago, the very idea of someone interrupting him would have been entirely unacceptable, but now it was an event he relished in mightily.

When Elizabeth noticed his steward arrive, she offered him a soft kiss, full of promise and enthusiasm, then rose and left the room to seek out Mrs. Reynolds. It was time the two began their preparations for the upcoming holiday festivities.

"Good morning, Mrs. Reynolds," Elizabeth practically sang as she entered the sitting room where the kind housekeeper was straightening a statue that rested on the mantle underneath an oil painting of Pemberley adorned in autumn colours.

"Good morning to you, too, Mrs. Darcy. What can I do for you this fine day?" Mrs. Reynolds turned, offering her full attention to her new mistress.

"As you know, my dear sister Jane and her new husband Mr. Bingley are expected on Saturday. Miss Darcy and the Colonel will arrive the day before that." Mrs. Reynolds acknowledged the information with a nod. "I would appreciate some of your time to discuss decorations we could place around the manor, as well as the menu while our guests are in residence."

"It would be my pleasure, Mrs. Darcy."

Elizabeth walked to the desk in the corner and took out a piece of paper, ink, and quill. Bringing them to the small table by the settee, the two sat and began planning the menu.

"I know my sister's tastes and preferences; however, I would like to know some of Fitz ...," she paused to amend how she addressed her husband in front of Mrs. Reynolds, "Mr. and Miss Darcy's preferred holiday dishes. After we speak about the food, I would then like to talk about the Darcy family traditions, as well as some decoration ideas." Elizabeth looked into Mrs. Reynolds's face and with all the seriousness she could muster she confided, "I depend upon you helping me make our first Christmas together perfect. I would be mortified if Mr. Darcy expected something and I did not provide it."

"Yes, ma'am, I would be happy to tell you all I know." Mrs. Reynolds smiled a warm, motherly smile as Elizabeth sat back and prepared to learn about her new family.

Mrs. Reynolds did not waste a minute, she began to speak animatedly about the Darcy siblings preferred foods and treats. The more she spoke about the Darcys, the clearer it became to Elizabeth that Mrs.

Reynolds loved the Darcy siblings as if they were her own children, and it clearly gave her immense pleasure to talk about them. It was exciting for Elizabeth to learn of her love's favourite dishes, and the more she listened, the more she understood how she could indulge her new sister's sweet tooth. Elizabeth would have never guessed Fitzwilliam liked caramel in his hot chocolate, or that Miss Darcy preferred marzipan to macaroons, but what mesmerized her most was Mrs. Reynolds's descriptions of their holiday traditions, so elaborate compared to anything she had ever experienced at Longbourn.

"The late Mr. and Mrs. Darcy enjoyed nothing more than a festive holiday. Many years ago, Mr. Darcy visited the Continent during Winter Solstice. He brought back with him the German tradition of a Christmas tree. He then incorporated the traditions of the Protestant reformer Martin Luther by wiring small candles to the tree. Mr. Darcy always said that the evergreen boughs reminded him of all of the green plants that would grow again once the frost was off the ground."

Elizabeth was entranced by every word

Mrs. Reynolds spoke; the tree, the candles, the decorations on the banisters, table centerpieces, and the exchange of trinkets. "This is all so fascinating. I have seen only one Christmas tree in my life. It must have been about five years ago when I visited my Aunt and Uncle Gardiner in London. One of the shops on Bond Street had a small tree sitting in the middle of a table. Though it was small, the memory of the tree has stayed with me. Where would we find a proper evergreen? Is there a tree upon the park grounds that would suffice?" Elizabeth's questions came in rapid succession, and Mrs. Reynolds smiled at her enthusiasm. An evergreen tree had not been brought into the manor and decorated since Lady Anne Darcy's death. The late Mr. Darcy had chosen to hide all of his emotions when his beloved wife died, to the detriment of his children, in her opinion. It was a shame because, although Fitzwilliam would remember, Georgiana would hardly recognize her family's little tradition; she was so young when her mother died.

"As luck would have it, we do have the perfect trees here upon the Pemberley grounds. The late Mr. Darcy had a grove of trees planted of the specific variety the

Germans use. It has been many years since the family has selected a tree, but the grove is still well maintained and there should be plenty to choose from." Elizabeth's enthusiasm was heightened with each proclamation from the beloved housekeeper. Mrs. Reynolds continued, "Her Ladyship would also decorate the most commonly used rooms and staircases with evergreen boughs lashed together. Mistletoe was hung in all the doorways, and a Yule log burned on Christmas Eve."

"A Yule log, oh, how glorious. My family has long practiced the Yule tradition, and I am glad we can continue it here." Elizabeth smiled sweetly and began sharing a part of her own family history with the housekeeper. "Every year my father would cut an oak branch and bore a hole in one end. My mother would make chrism by mixing wine, cooking oil, and incense. The chrism was added to the log and the hole plugged, then my sisters and I would wrap the log in the most glorious white linen and lace. On Christmas Eve, my father would say a prayer over the log and we would burn it all night. Christmas morning, all of my father's tenants would gather, and my father would offer another prayer of blessing over every household under his care, as well as the coming year's crops. In the spring, the ashes would be spread over the fields. It is believed that our family, the tenants, and crops will all be blessed with health and bounty."

Mrs. Reynolds enjoyed listening to her new mistress share her family traditions. The two were nearing the end of their conversation and dividing the tasks when Fitzwilliam was noticed leaning against the doorway, watching his wife. *That man will never tire of watching his wife,* thought Mrs. Reynolds.

Fitzwilliam nodded a greeting to the ladies when they saw him at the door. Mrs. Reynolds stood, curtsied, and then stepped out of his way so he could take her position on the settee next to his wife.

"Nay, Mrs. Reynolds, you remain. I am just come to tell Elizabeth that I have completed my business and will await her in the library." Fitzwilliam walked towards the settee. As he gained Elizabeth's side he rested his hand upon her shoulder in a show of affection. Elizabeth looked up at him and, to her shock, in front of Mrs. Reynolds and without a care in the world, he bent over and kissed her sweet lips. He kissed her as a man kisses his wife, then he licked her taste from his own lips and stood erect. He straightened his vest and said, "Please join me in the library when you have completed your planning." Fitzwilliam had started to walk away when his wife addressed him.

"Fitzwilliam, you should join us. We are almost done planning, but it would be wonderful if you would accompany me to select the Christmas tree and Yule log."

"Very well, my dear." He pulled a high-backed chair close to the settee so he could sit near Elizabeth without making Mrs. Reynolds abandon her position.

The actual planning only took a few more minutes, but now that the three were together much of the following hour was spent reminiscing about past holidays. Although their time together exceeded what was required to accomplish their tasks, it was to the enjoyment of them all.

# Chapter 2

It had been decided that Fitzwilliam and Elizabeth would take the sleigh and ride out to find the Christmas tree and Yule log posthaste. Nothing could deter them from their task, not even the icy temperatures of the north of England. They were determined to find the perfect tree. Dressed in the warmest clothes they could muster, they stepped into their horse-drawn sleigh, placing heating stones at their feet and warm blankets over their laps. Elizabeth's eyes were glowing with the pleasure of adventuring out of doors with her new husband.

Although her family owned a sleigh, Elizabeth rarely went out in it. Hertfordshire was far enough south that the winter weather brought more rain than snow, and as a result they experienced mostly mud. When there was snow on the ground her mother's palpitations ran rampant, and all five of her daughters were required to remain with her, confining Elizabeth to the house far longer than she preferred.

Once they were comfortably situated, Fitzwilliam snapped the reins and they set out at a trot over the snowy path. A gardener followed the Darcys' sleigh with a cargo sled so the tree could be brought back with them. He also carried the necessary tools they would need to fell the tree.

The Pemberley grounds were extensive, more than 1,500 acres for the manor, gardens, and crops, not to mention the tenants' homesteads and fields. In all, Mr. Darcy was responsible for the lands encompassing a full ten miles. The farther they rode the more in awe of her husband Elizabeth became; for a man so young to be responsible for so many people! The idea of such a man loving her warmed her heart. Wrapping her arm through his, she snuggled close to him.

Much of their journey was spent with Elizabeth listening while Fitzwilliam pointed out elements of interest on the estate grounds. He entertained her with stories of his youth frequently consisting of himself being led around by his cousin Richard, constantly getting into some mischief or other. She loved hearing his tales of adventure and easily understood the everlasting bond of not only familial love, but of friendship that the two had for one another.

Finally, Fitzwilliam slowed the sleigh at the edge of a grove of trees. The trees ranged in size from no more than knee-high to trees towering a full thirty feet. Looking at the expanse in front of them, Fitzwilliam explained. "My father had this grove of Evergreens planted the year he returned from the Continent. Some of them have been here more than twenty years, the others much less. You see, these trees are not native to our region, and so particular attention must be taken to grow them successfully."

Elizabeth looked around in awe. Many of the trees she had never laid eyes on before; they were a rare sight to be seen. "However will we choose one?"

Stepping out of the sleigh, he offered Elizabeth his hand and helped her down. "Easy; we will walk around and look at them. When we have found the perfect tree, my man will chop it down and return it to the house for us."

At that moment the two were walking past a particularly large tree, and Elizabeth let out a small gasp. "Do you think it will fit in the house?"

Chuckling softly, Fitzwilliam teased, "If not, we will simply have the roof removed for the season. I think it can be restored easily enough next spring." Seeing the laughter in his eyes as he spoke to her, Elizabeth swatted at his arm with her gloved hand. Turning serious, he said, "Let us look for a smaller tree. This one is far too tall. There are plenty more that will fit inside just fine."

The next hour was spent rambling through the grove selecting a glorious tree and Yule log. When at last the gardener had it chopped down and Fitzwilliam had helped him fix it to the sled, he was sent back to the manor with his load. Elizabeth and Fitzwilliam regained their sleigh, and the two set their return course to the manor. Rather than return the way they had come, they took a more leisurely path leading them around the grove and landing them at the westernmost façade of the manor, near the Orangery. Elizabeth took in the sight of the magnificent structure covered in its fantastic winter wrapping. "Oh, Fitzwilliam, please stop the sleigh. I must get out and take in this majestic scene before me."

Fitzwilliam did as she requested, and for the second time the two stepped out to enjoy the sight together. He explained the architectural details of the Italian structure, his pride in his ancestral home visible in the features of his face. After standing in the same place for five minutes a shiver of cold coursed through him. "Come, Elizabeth, it is time we returned to the house. I fear we will develop a cold if we stay out here too long." Fitzwilliam turned towards the sleigh, but Elizabeth dropped his arm and took a few steps forward. She sighed at the sight before her; she could scarcely believe she was the mistress of Pemberley.

Elizabeth began walking towards the sleigh. Fitzwilliam had turned his attention towards adjusting the reins on the horse, and Elizabeth took full advantage of his distracted state. She bent over and scooped up a large handful of snow and compacted it into a snowball. Launching the offending object with her right arm, she giggled as it hit Fitzwilliam's back with a thud. He turned to look at her, but she was already preparing a second ball which she expertly launched at him. It struck him square in the chest, cold bits of snow flying into his face as it broke apart. He looked down at the clumps of snow clinging to his coat. With a roar he lunged at Elizabeth and gently tackled her, pulling her with him to the ground.

Elizabeth screeched at his actions but enjoyed rolling through the snow with him. She grabbed handfuls and unceremoniously threw them at him, an action he reciprocated. Their lighthearted playing only lasted a minute or two then, as Elizabeth was about to launch another round of snow at him, Fitzwilliam caught her hand and pulled her towards him. They were lying on the ground, their wool coats, hats, scarves, and gloves coated with clumps of snow. Flurries of snow flitted through the air around them. At first Elizabeth struggled against him, determined to win their little snow fight, until her eyes met Fitzwilliam's. His were dark pools of love, and at once she was lost in them. Pulling her tight against him, he kissed her lips. Her lips were just as cold as his, but neither hesitated. Rather they warmed themselves with their shared passion. Had Elizabeth been able to think, she certainly would have wondered why the snow they lay upon had not melted with their combined heat. Fitzwilliam's body shuddered against Elizabeth, reacting as any man violently in love would. Their kiss became more passionate until they both shared the taste and essence of the other. Elizabeth sighed into Fitzwilliam; the sound was almost lost upon the wind, but Fitzwilliam heard it and pulled Elizabeth closer, deepening their kiss. Elizabeth's cold nose brushed against his as the warmth of their combined breaths sent puffs of vapor into the air around them. Wrapping both arms around her, Fitzwilliam luxuriated in the blissful sensation of having his wife so near him. Though their bodies were wet and cold, neither felt it, for they were on fire with desire.

Drawing a deep breath, Fitzwilliam spoke first. "Elizabeth, let us go back to the house this instant." Then, letting his breath out, he whispered against her ear, "I need you, most ardently."

Elizabeth gasped and caught his lips in a final kiss before rising from the cold, snowy ground. They quickly settled into the sleigh and rode back to the manor. Pulling up in front of the house, they were met by a groom who took the reins of the horse and returned it and the sleigh to the stables. He shook his head at the mess he had just witnessed, his master and mistress returning to the house with clumps of snow clinging to every part of them as if they had rolled around on the ground like little children.

Mr. Carson smiled as he poured the last bucket of hot water into the bath for Mr. Darcy. He doubted the bath would be used, as the master frequented his wife's bath as often as he used his own, but still he prepared it. He had seen the two coming up the road and knew they would be cold after such a length of time outdoors in this weather. *What better way to warm up than a bath,* he thought. Gracie had already filled her mistress's bath and was just finishing laying out her clothing. The two beloved servants had already learned that once the master's and mistress's baths were drawn and their belongings laid out for the night, they were rarely needed again; today would be no different.

Fitzwilliam and Elizabeth had returned to the manor in a fit of untidiness. Their outer clothing was caked with snow, their clothing underneath cold and wet, yet neither complained. Mrs. Darcy's hair was loose from her bonnet, wet strands sticking to the sides of her face as she cast off the soaked layers of her scarf, gloves, and coat.

The two had tried to remain composed in the company of the household staff, but as soon as the door to the master suite closed, all propriety was dismissed. Gracie had already departed the room, but Mr. Carson was still in the washroom when he heard them enter. It was obvious neither could remove their own clothing, or that of the other, quick enough. Mr. Carson left the room via the servants' staircase at the back of the washroom. Rarely had the man ever used the door when it was only Mr. Darcy he served. However, with the new Mrs. Darcy in residence he was finding that it was becoming his preferred method of coming and going so as not to disturb the young couple who were so obviously in love.

Fitzwilliam was captivated with the velvety skin of Elizabeth's neck. Their bodies were numb from the cold of their excursion, but there were pockets of warmth both were enjoying the opportunity to discover. He kissed her, starting at her lips and slowly working his way to her ankles and back up. By the time he reached her lips a second time, both were well within the throes of passion and could no longer resist the desire to be one as only a husband and wife should be.

Neither Fitzwilliam nor Elizabeth were seen again for the rest of the day.

# Chapter 3

The preparations of the week were coming to a conclusion, and already Friday was nigh. Elizabeth and Mrs. Reynolds had worked endlessly to decorate the manor, plan the meals, and get everything in general order. Their efforts had paid off; the manor looked exquisite. The staircases were draped with boughs of evergreen and red satin ribbon. There were matching evergreen centerpieces with candles scattered throughout the manor. A sprig of mistletoe tied with a small ribbon hung in every doorway. The main sitting room had been re-arranged to accommodate the tree that had been cut from the grove. All that was left was to go over the final menu with the cook, decorate the tree, and make the chrism to fill the Yule log. Elizabeth had had the gardener bore the hole in the log earlier in the week, and her white silk and satin wrappings were already prepared.

Between Elizabeth and Mrs. Reynolds there was nothing else to be done. Their family party of six, plus Georgiana's companion, Mrs. Annesley, if she chose to join them, would have a remarkably comfortable holiday enjoying each other's good nature and friendship.

The wind had begun to blow from the west, causing a cold chill the stableman feared would be too much for some of the livestock. Fitzwilliam had been called to offer his advice less than an hour after the midday repast. He told Elizabeth it was likely he would be riding out with the servant to bring in the livestock from the fields. His description of the severe cold worried her not only for his safety and that of their livestock, but also for the safety of their guests travelling over the harsh winter roads.

Colonel Fitzwilliam and Georgiana were due tomorrow, with the Bingleys right behind them the following day. Elizabeth wanted nothing more than for all of them to arrive safe and sound before the weather took a turn for the worse. It could become dismal after they were all securely ensconced at Pemberley, but not before.

Elizabeth stood at the sitting room window, looking out across the long drive both of her beloved sisters would soon be travelling up. She tried to dwell on the positive, but she feared the bitter cold would ruin all of their plans to be together. Elizabeth offered up a silent prayer for their safety.

A few minutes later, Elizabeth was still standing at the frost-glazed window looking out across the expanse in front of her. She was feeling a little insignificant and alone when she saw an express rider coming towards the manor. He was hunched in the saddle with the brim of his hat pulled down to protect him from the icy wind. When he neared the manor and then disappeared by the servants' entrance she gave up her spot and instead sat down and took up her book. It was but a few minutes before Mrs. Reynolds entered with a tray of tea.

"A letter for you, Mrs. Darcy. It just arrived express."

Elizabeth thanked Mrs. Reynolds, who began to pour the tea while she opened her letter. She smiled when she realized it was a letter from her sister Jane.

*Dearest Lizzy,*

*How I miss you. It brings me absolute joy that we will soon be joined again for the Christmas season. I am sure by the time you receive this our arrival will be imminent, but I could never live with myself if you were surprised entirely. Just this morning Mamma informed me she, Papa, Mary, and Kitty will be accompanying us to Pemberley for Christmas. Not only that, dear sister, but we are leaving a full day and a half before we had intended. I fear you should expect us no later than Thursday, the nineteenth of December. We can only guess our time of arrival, but Charles tells me it will be around three o'clock in the afternoon.*

*All my love,*

*Jane*

Looking at the clock on the mantle

Elizabeth panicked when she realized today was Thursday, and already it was nearing three o'clock. If Charles's prediction was correct, the Bingleys and Bennets would be arriving any minute.

Elizabeth's face was pale, and she was near panic when she addressed her housekeeper. "Mrs. Reynolds."

"Yes, ma'am," the housekeeper calmly responded.

"I have just received this letter. It seems all our well-made plans are about to be upset. My sister Jane Bingley writes that not only is she and Charles to be arriving, but my whole family is to be joining them." She paused to catch her breath a little and the kind housekeeper tried to put her at ease.

"Very well, Mrs. Darcy, we will modify accordingly. Is there anything else?"

Elizabeth stood a little agitated, but she replied, "Yes, there is one more thing. Apparently they left Longbourn early."

"How early?"

"To the best of my knowledge, they left a day and a half early, meaning the appearance of their carriage is expected any minute. I suspect we will need to amend tonight's menu, as well as prepare two, possibly three, more rooms. My sisters Mary and Kitty may share a room if needed."

"Nonsense, Mrs. Darcy. We have plenty of rooms, and all of them can be prepared at a moment's notice. I will send Abigail up now to ensure they are ready."

"Oh, Mrs. Reynolds, you know not how you have eased my mind."

"Will there be anything else, Mrs. Darcy?"

"No, that is all."

"Very well, I will get right to work."

No sooner had Mrs. Reynolds turned to leave than the door opened to admit the butler. "Mrs. Darcy, I am come to inform you there is an unknown carriage coming up the drive. They should be here in about ten minutes."

"Thank you," Elizabeth responded and then turned to Mrs. Reynolds. "It appears as if they are already here." Elizabeth quickly glanced at her gown and then raised her eyebrows. She cleared her throat with a bit of hesitation. "Ahem, Mrs. Reynolds, there is perhaps one more thing you should know."

Mrs. Reynolds looked at her nervous mistress. She had not yet witnessed Mrs. Darcy in such a state and felt sorry for the dear lady.

"You see," she paused trying to choose the right words, "my mother has a tendency to be quite vocal. Please understand she always means well, but sometimes she does not think before she speaks."

"I understand, Mrs. Darcy. Fear not, everyone has a member of their family they wish would restrain themselves. Why, my own mother was a bit eccentric at times. Now, if you will excuse me, I will set things in motion and return before the guests reach the house."

Elizabeth appreciated the woman's kindness, and for the second time in a space of no more than ten minutes Elizabeth stood at the window and watched the progression of her visitors. When the carriage reached the house, she waited in the foyer with Mrs. Reynolds while the footman and butler helped her family enter the manor. She did not even have time to receive them properly before her mother blurted out, "Goodness, Lord bless me, look at your house, Lizzy. I daresay this place is as large as a palace. I knew Mr. Darcy was wealthy, but for heaven's sake, he must be the richest man in England. At least now I need not worry for the death of your father. Your Mr. Darcy is certainly able to take care of me, even if Mr. Bingley cannot."

Elizabeth looked around at the stoic faces of Mrs. Reynolds and the butler. Mrs. Reynolds had been properly warned, but no one else knew what to expect from her mother. It was obvious the butler had thought he would meet a refined and sophisticated woman, considering Elizabeth and Mrs. Gardiner, whom he remembered from last summer's tour.

"Mamma," Elizabeth said with irritation in her voice. It was then that her father stepped forward and addressed her.

"Elizabeth, how are you, my dear?" He opened his arms and welcomed her into his embrace.

"I am well, Father. How was your journey?"

"It was as I expected it would be, travelling such a distance with, dare I say, three silly women. Jane and Charles did aid me along the way when they offered me a place of refuge in their carriage."

Elizabeth looked around before responding, "Where is Jane and Charles? Are they not with you?"

"Oh, they will be along shortly. Charles

wanted to show Jane the view from a peak a few miles off."

Mrs. Bennet voiced her opinion on the matter. "The view ... pft. I know not what Charles was thinking. Jane will catch her death traipsing around some peak in this frigid weather, just to take in a view. He should not have stopped the coach, but rather continued right behind us." She quickly swung her head to look at the hall around her, then continued before she hardly had time to take a breath. "Well, Lizzy, what a lovely place you have here. Your home is quite festive. Jane has always been a better decorator than you, but I like this exceedingly well indeed. I guess scolding you until you got it right paid off after all, though it is likely your staff did most of the decorating. How could they not? I expect you must have at least one hundred servants in the house alone."

Elizabeth was mortified, "Yes, Mamma, Fitzwilliam's staff is wonderfully adept. So much so that with nothing more than ten minutes' notice your rooms have been prepared. Perhaps you would like to see them now?" Then addressing her sisters for the first time, she invited them also. "What say you, Mary and Kitty? Would you like to see your rooms?" The girls nodded in unison, though neither said a word. Elizabeth was happy they had sense enough to hold their tongues. The same could not be said for her mother.

"Oh yes, my dear, show me to my room. After such a journey you know how tired I am. Nothing would suit me more than lying down for a spell. Indeed, I must rest my poor feet. Why, the only way I could be more tired was if I had actually walked the distance myself." Mrs. Bennet was already following the footman who carried her trunks.

Mr. Bennet looked upon his daughter and then whispered as he turned to follow his wife, "Thank you, Lizzy. I am sorry we have surprised you so, but you know your mother. There was no stopping her once she learned Jane was to come to Pemberley. I thought it best that I accompany her, rather than let her come alone."

"It is fine, Father. I am glad you have come."

Mr. Bennet planted a kiss on Elizabeth's forehead and followed his wife and daughters up the stairs.

Elizabeth let out her breath and turned to

face Mrs. Reynolds and the butler. She started to apologize, but Mrs. Reynolds stopped her with a statement of understanding. "There is no need to speak, Mrs. Darcy. I think I know what you are going to say. Trust me, we all have family members we sometimes want to apologize for, but there is no need. Now, if you will excuse me, I will go and help Cook."

Mrs. Reynolds left Elizabeth, who returned to the sitting room to watch for her sister. A few minutes later the butler returned and addressed her. "Mrs. Darcy, I have been sent to inform you that another carriage was spotted coming up the drive. We are to understand it is Mr. Bingley's carriage."

"Thank you," Elizabeth responded. "Have word sent to Mr. Darcy that the Bingleys have arrived, and tell him also that the Bennets have accompanied them."

"Very well. Will there be anything else?"

"No, that is all."

The butler left Elizabeth alone looking out the window for a third time that day, watching the progress of another carriage coming up the drive. Elizabeth was eager to see her sister again, and the slow progress of the carriage did nothing but frustrate her.

Finally, the carriage pulled up in front of the house and Elizabeth rushed out the door into the waiting arms of her sister who had just been handed down.

"Oh, Jane, how I have missed you."

"I have missed you, too, Lizzy. Did you get my letter? Were you properly warned in advance of our parents and sisters' arrival?"

"As much as could have been expected in this weather. I think the letter arrived about half an hour ago."

"Half an hour! I am sorry, Lizzy. I hoped it would have arrived yesterday."

"Speak no more of it. Come, let us go inside and get warm. Your trip must have been unbearable in this weather."

"It was not quite as dire as that. It is vastly preferable to travel with one's husband than one's family. Charles was aptly able to keep me warm the entire journey." Jane blushed a little as she spoke, looking over her shoulder towards her new husband, Charles.

Elizabeth understood her sister's meaning. Gripping her hand, she pulled her into the house, exclaiming over her shoulder, "Come in, Charles, you are welcome. Fitzwilliam will be along any minute. He has been attending some estate business today, but I have already sent word of your arrival."

Stepping into the foyer, Elizabeth helped Jane remove her outerwear. "Oh, Lizzy, your home is beautiful. Look at the glorious decorations." Jane took in the view of the place, enjoying everything she saw.

"Thank you. I must admit Mrs. Reynolds, our housekeeper, is the one you should compliment. She has an extraordinary gift for turning any object into a beautiful work of art."

Just then, Charles came bounding through the door, as amiable as he always was. "Elizabeth, what a pleasure it is to see you again." He enveloped her in a hug anyone would enjoy from a favourite brother; both laughed light-heartedly.

"It is a pleasure to see you, too, Charles. I cannot thank you enough for bringing my sister here for Christmas."

"Pish-posh, think nothing of it. It is us that should thank you for inviting us. Jane was eager to come, not only to see her favourite sister, but to see your home. I have been telling her all about the beauty of Pemberley and the surrounding area."

"For my part, I cannot but agree with

you. Thus far I have found Aunt Gardiner's statement last summer to be exact. She declared Derbyshire to be the most majestic county." Jane and Charles nodded in agreement with Elizabeth's assessment. "Our parents told me you stopped at the peaks to see the view. Did you like it?" Elizabeth asked.

Jane smiled shyly and then looked to her husband, who nodded again. Jane turned in her chair and reached for Elizabeth's hands, which she held in her own. "Lizzy, Charles and I did not stop *just* to witness the view; we were looking down upon a particular piece of property." Elizabeth's eyes grew wide, but she sat quietly while her sister continued. "In just these few short weeks married, I have determined that a woman may be settled too near her family. Charles and I have decided that we will not extend the lease at Netherfield, but instead Charles's solicitor has found us a property here in the north, closer to Pemberley. I must admit, I have missed you dearly, and since Charles and Fitzwilliam are such loyal friends there could not be a better place for us than an estate nearby." Jane was rambling a bit, but Elizabeth loved it. She knew her sister well enough to know she only rambled when she cared whether the person she was speaking to agreed with her decision. She too often tried to defend herself, but it was not needed. Elizabeth was extremely excited at her sister's news.

"Oh, Jane, do you speak the truth? Nothing would make me happier than having you settled close. Where is it? How far off will you be?"

Jane laughed at her sisters delight. "It is but seven miles from here. Just two miles on the other side of Lambton."

"So near! Why, Jane, I am so excited." Then, turning more serious, she asked, "Does our family know?"

Jane portrayed a sternness Elizabeth had never before witnessed in her. "No, and you will not tell them either. Mamma has not left us alone, not one single day since we married. I suspect she will not be happy, but we do not care. She is interrupting our life too much. I have spoken with father about asking her to visit less, but it has had no effect. Her constant visits are a disruption to my new home. How am I to earn the respect of the household when Mamma is constantly telling them to do things differently than me? It is too much, and already I am tired."

"Dear Jane, how much you have had to endure. I am sorry. Here I have been enjoying wedded bliss, and you have had nothing but grief."

"Do not worry, Lizzy, it has not been all bad. Charles and I have been quite happy getting to know one another." Jane blushed again and looked down at their hands still clasped in a sisterly bond.

The three talked amiably for more than an hour until Elizabeth witnessed Jane's stifled yawn.

"Come, we must let you rest. I will take you up and then I must speak with Mrs. Reynolds and our cook. Mrs. Reynolds assured me the added guests are no burden, but I still worry. We have quadrupled our company, and on a day no one was expected." Jane tried to apologize again, but Elizabeth would hear none of it. She stood and led them from the room just as Fitzwilliam was briskly coming up the hall towards them.

"Elizabeth, I am sorry I have been gone so long. I see your sister and Charles are here. Is it true your parents and younger sisters are here too?"

Elizabeth reached up on her toes and greeted him with a kiss upon his cold cheek. "It is true. They are already in their rooms, resting. I am just sending Jane and Charles up."

Fitzwilliam and Charles grasped hands pounded each other on their backs, a brotherly embrace the women had often witnessed during the months of their engagements and wedding. It warmed the hearts of Elizabeth and Jane to know they had found husbands that were best friends and as close as two brothers ever could be.

A few more greetings were exchanged then Charles led Jane to their room. A guide was not necessary once Elizabeth explained they would share the room Charles normally occupied during his previous visits to Pemberley.

Elizabeth sent Fitzwilliam to freshen up with a promise that she would be along shortly to change for supper. She then called upon Mrs. Reynolds and confirmed the meal was well under control.

Looking at the clock on the wall as she left the housekeeper's room, Elizabeth was well pleased that she had time to call upon her sisters Mary and Catherine, whom everyone called Kitty.

"I hope you enjoyed your trip, Mary," Elizabeth said when Mary opened the door and allowed her in. Mary had a beautiful room that overlooked the garden paths below. The walls were covered with an ivory paper with little pink and yellow flowers. The curtains were a thick, dark brown material that aptly blocked the morning sun. The furnishings were lovely, though not overdone as they were in so many houses in England. Elizabeth already appreciated the simplicity of the Darcys' impeccable taste and style. It was a design she could easily find comfort in.

"Yes, it was a fine journey, though one none of us expected." Mary looked at her sister with an air of suspicion. She knew that inviting themselves to Pemberley was not proper, but secretly she was glad they had come. She had kept her ears tuned to every conversation regarding the place and had been anxious to see it in person.

"I am glad it was tolerable for you. The weather is quite cold and the roads rough. When I heard you were all coming I feared it would be a little too much."

"As you can imaging, a carriage with three fewer sisters is a great deal more comfortable for extended travel."

Elizabeth laughed softly at her sister's reaction. "I can well believe that." Offering her sister a hug, she said, "I am glad you are here, Mary. My first Christmas away from Longbourn will be more bearable with so many of my family here."

Mary returned Elizabeth's hug and, not with a little reluctance, confessed her feelings, "With three sisters recently married, there have been many changes at Longbourn. I must admit, I was feeling a bit despondent as we began decorating the house. It is very lonely without you, Jane, and Lydia."

Elizabeth hugged her sister tighter, offering what little comfort she could. The two understood one another perfectly. Elizabeth released her and turned towards the door. She opened it, but before she left she addressed her once more. "Supper will be at six o'clock. I will see you there, Mary."

Next, Elizabeth sought out Kitty's room. The moment Kitty's door opened Elizabeth could feel the excitement exuding from her young sister. Kitty was seventeen, but sometimes Elizabeth wondered if she had aged at all since twelve. Kitty reached out and gripped Elizabeth's hand. Pulling her into the room, she exclaimed, "Oh, Lizzy, what a splendid house you have. I have never seen such a gorgeous place. May I come and stay with you often? I think my new brother must have lots of rich friends. I am confident I could come stay here and meet some pleasant men."

"We will see, Kitty," was all Elizabeth could get out before her sister spoke again.

"I hope you have gotten me a fine present."

"I did; however, they were sent to Longbourn just this week. It is likely you passed them en route."

"Oh, fiddlesticks! I guess we will just have to see what you have that I want." Elizabeth was shocked at her sisters audacity. "La, Lizzy, you cannot expect me not to open any presents Christmas morning."

"Kitty!" Elizabeth scolded.

"What? You know as well as I how much I enjoy receiving presents. Well, it does not matter much anyway. Our presents from Lydia arrived, and I am sure she knows me better than anyone else; she will have bought me something I am certain to love."

Elizabeth rolled her eyes at her silly sister, gave her a quick hug, and turned towards the door before informing her of supper as she had done their sister Mary.

Finally, Elizabeth stopped at their parents' room. She hesitantly knocked upon their door. Her father answered. He looked tired and worn, but when his eyes saw her they lit up like they always did.

"Ah, Lizzy, you have come to check on us. I assure you all is well. Your mother adores her room. In fact, she wonders if the King himself has stayed in it. She likes it so much that twice already she has tried to seek out Mr. Darcy to inform him of her approval." He smiled wryly as he continued, "I assured her she could pay him her compliments at supper." He winked at Elizabeth as her mother was heard in the background.

"Oh yes, tell Mr. Darcy how marvelous it is. Why, look here," she swung her arm, beckoning Elizabeth to enter. "He has had everything made up just right for us. We have these wonderfully soft towels, lovely smelling soaps and salts, as well as pen and ink should we care to write a letter. Our trunks were brought up by the smartest servants, and already he has had your lovely housekeeper send me flowers from the Orangery. What a good son-in-law he is."

Elizabeth looked around. It was just as her mother said. There on the table in front of her was a lovely display of all the flowers she had just seen in bloom when they last visited the place. She was proud of Fitzwilliam's thoughtfulness and was glad her mother was satisfied with her situation.

"I am sure Fitzwilliam will be more than happy to accept your compliments at supper. As it is, supper is nearing and I still need to dress. Please excuse me. I will see you in the drawing room at six o'clock."

"Oh yes, Lizzy, make sure you put on your red dress. It is quite festive and looks so well with your hair. I am sure your Mr. Darcy will approve."

"Mamma," Elizabeth scolded as she held the door open, ready to leave, "I need not wear a specific gown to catch my husband's approval. He and I are already married. Besides, he approves of all my gowns."

"Do not be so sure, Lizzy. You have only been married a few short weeks, and Mr. Darcy does not yet have an heir. You had best retain his notice, or he is apt to send you packing and find himself a better wife."

"Mother!"

"Now, Lizzy, do not over-react at your mother's silly musings. You know as well as I that she is slightly mad. Go get yourself dressed. We will see you at supper." Mr. Bennet shut the door behind Elizabeth, who stood in place for a moment while the fury within her subsided. In the past, the little tiffs she overheard between her parents had never brought her any pleasure, but now as she leaned her head near the door and heard her father scold her mother, she felt a little better.

Elizabeth entered the master suite and stepped through the sitting room doors into the adjacent rooms. She saw Fitzwilliam stepping out of his warm bath. Her eyes roamed his body and she sucked in a deep breath, remembering every sensation she had experienced in their few weeks of wedded bliss. A sultry smile crossed her lips when she saw him react under her watchful gaze.

"Fitzwilliam, you are a handsome man. I could look at you all day."

"I am glad you think so, my dear."

He reached for a towel and dried his body. Elizabeth stepped to her vanity and watched him in the mirror while she removed her earrings and necklace. His shoulders flexed as he reached behind to grip the towel and dry his back. When he raised his arm to dry his neck and hair the musculature of his abdomen rippled. She truly appreciated his body.

"Thank you for sending my mother flowers. She cannot stop prattling about how wonderful they are."

"Flowers? Oh, I told Mrs. Reynolds this week to make sure Jane was sent a spray. She must have had another put together for your mother. Very good, I will make sure I thank her for that. Mrs. Reynolds is a saint; she never misses anything. You will see, my dear. No matter what, she will make sure everything goes off without a hitch. Our holiday will be perfect, even with this unexpected increase in the number of guests."

"I am sure you are right, but you know I cannot help but worry something frightful will happen. It is in my nature."

Reaching behind her back, Elizabeth unbuttoned the top three buttons of her gown. Seeing her struggling, Fitzwilliam stepped over and helped her with the rest. "As much as I adore helping you dress and undress," his eyes met hers in the mirror, "you should consider allowing Gracie to come help you more while everyone is here. I can already tell you will be over-extending yourself; her assistance will likely be a relief."

"I know I should call her in, but she will change everything. You will no longer be able to remain here with me, sharing conversation while we prepare."

Fitzwilliam chuckled, but he agreed. "You do have a point." He wrapped his arms round her and bent low to kiss her neck. Elizabeth melted into his arms.

"It may not be preferred by either of us, but it is likely the most rational decision. We do not have to maintain this state forever, just until everyone leaves again. Here, I will call her while you rinse in the tub."

Elizabeth smiled at the retreating figure of her husband, now dressed in his robe and house slippers. He certainly was a man of action.

Elizabeth finished undressing, stepped over the side of the ornate tub, and immersed herself in the warm, sudsy water. She was not dirty enough to require a bath, but the warm water was already there. Why should she not indulge for a few minutes? Elizabeth's head was leaning against the curve of the tub, her eyes closed, when Gracie entered and began silently preparing a few of her mistress's items.

Elizabeth had interviewed five lady's maids her second week at Pemberley, Fitzwilliam had all but insisted she select a maid and have one ready should she need her services. Elizabeth liked all of the girls, but Gracie stood out from the rest with her smile that did not just linger on her lips but rather lit up her entire being. Elizabeth was sure the two would get along splendidly.

Hearing movement in the room around her, Elizabeth opened her eyes and noticed Gracie. "Gracie, you have come. Thank you for attending me on such short notice."

Gracie discontinued the task of setting out her mistress's clothing and turned all of her attention to Elizabeth. "It is my pleasure, Mrs. Darcy. Do you have a specific gown you prefer tonight or should I make a selection for you?"

"My mother has arrived and all but demanded I wear my crimson gown, but I was saving it for Christmas morning." Elizabeth let out a sigh, "What do you recommend? Do I have another that will do in its place? My hope is not to garner my mother's wrath. In order to avoid it, I need a gown that is sophisticated enough to retain my husband's attention until I have produced him an heir."

Gracie stood, staring at her mistress, unable to respond to such a statement.

"Do not look at me that way. You have not met my mother. I am not mocking her when I speak so; she honestly believes Mr. Darcy will soon lose interest in me."

"Mrs. Darcy, if I may be so bold, I doubt very highly the master will lose interest in you. I have never seen a man so devoted to a woman."

"That is what I think, too. I am sure he loves me as much as I do him. There is no chance I will put him away, rather I would marry him again in a heartbeat," Elizabeth gaily responded.

"I think you should wear your green velvet gown. I know its design is simple, but with the right shawl, hair accessories, and jewellery, we can make it every bit as stunning."

"I agree. The green gown it is."

Elizabeth stood up and then stepped over

the edge of the tub, accepting the offered towel. Gracie helped her dry and then held the dressing gown for her. Elizabeth picked up her hairbrush and sat down upon the chair near the fire to brush out her hair while she waited for Gracie to finish setting out her attire. She had been careful not to get her hair wet in the tub, but there were a few strands that had come loose from the simple bun she had fashioned high on her head and gotten wet.

"I have your clothing articles prepared, Mrs. Darcy." Gracie curtsied as she addressed her mistress.

"I am coming," Elizabeth stood reluctantly; she was not looking forward to a meal with her entire family. She had planned this evening to be special. The last night of privacy with her husband before their guests arrived.

Gracie did not know her mistress well, but each time she waited on her she learned a little more of her lighthearted playfulness. Tonight it was not as prevalent as it had been in the past, but rather had a sense of bitter sarcasm. Gracie remained silent as she set about her task of dressing Elizabeth for supper.

They were nearing completion when there was a knock upon the door.

"It is open," Elizabeth called over her shoulder.

Fitzwilliam opened the door and stepped into Elizabeth's room. "You look lovely, my dear. I love that dark green colour upon you. It reminds me of a particular outing we recently experienced when we were out looking for an *evergreen*." His eyes sought hers and she noticed his roguish smile.

Elizabeth glanced at her maid, who normally would have considered the comment innocent except she noticed the blush upon her mistress's cheeks, neck, and chest. Gracie continued to arrange Elizabeth's hair, trying to act as if she did not realize her master had even entered the room.

"I am glad you like it. You may as well know my mother all but demanded I wear my red gown. Be prepared to listen to her *opinion* on the matter when we go below stairs."

"I do not care what your mother thinks, and neither should you."

Elizabeth let out a snort-laugh that reminded Gracie of one of the barnyard animals. She looked upon her mistress's face, a little shocked at first, but when it did not faze the lady, she relaxed and delighted that the mistress was finally at ease enough to enjoy herself. The master certainly did not mind. "Pft ... not care! Oh, I do not care what she thinks. I never have. What I care about is what she *says*, and who she says it in front of. It is her manner that disturbs me."

"Elizabeth, do not dramatize your mother's theatrics. It is just going to be us, your family, Richard, and Georgiana here for Christmas. Certainly with all of us being so close, and already understanding your mother's antics, we can pass the holiday with little tribulation."

"I hope you are right," she said aloud, but the truth was she doubted his words.

Gracie finished Elizabeth's hair and picked up the shawl for her mistress. Placing it on her shoulders, she asked, "What time should I come help you prepare for bed, Mrs. Darcy?"

"That will not be necessary, Gracie. Simply lay out my nightgown, robe, and slippers. I will be able to undress myself. If I have trouble, Mr. Darcy will help me."

"I certainly shall," Fitzwilliam responded as he offered Elizabeth his arm.

Now it was Gracie's turn to blush. She bowed her head low as her mistress left the room on the arm of the master.

# Chapter 4

The Darcys were the first below stairs. They took advantage of the lack of guests to meet with Mrs. Reynolds. Elizabeth was relieved when she was told that Mrs. Lacroix, Pemberley's cook, had pulled off a lovely meal with such short notice.

Mid-discussion, all three jerked their heads towards the sound of shattering glass and screaming. The three instantly fled the room towards the staircase at the center of the manor. Fitzwilliam led the way, his long strides getting him there swiftly.

"It is your fault, Kitty. If you had not pushed me, none of this would have happened," Mary accused her younger sister.

"Pushed you! Why, I did not push you. How dare you insinuate this mess is in any way my responsibility?"

"But it is. You are the one who came

barreling out of your room and pushed me into the table."

"Mary, I cannot believe that you, of all people, would resort to lying at a time such as this. Tell the truth."

"That is the truth."

"ENOUGH!" Fitzwilliam shouted over the noise of the arguing sisters. "Tell me what happened this instant."

Both of the girls began speaking over one another. Each told their version of the events as their voices drowned each other out, until both were nearly shouting to be heard. Neither Elizabeth nor Fitzwilliam could make any sense out of their shouting. It was obvious both of them blamed the other and neither intended to accept responsibility.

"Mary, Kitty, lower your voices this instant. For heaven's sake, are you infants to be squalling so?" Elizabeth's scolding quieted Mary, but Kitty would not stop.

"But Elizabeth, it was not ...," Kitty protested, her voice still raised.

Fitzwilliam put up a hand to quiet her, but it did not work. His nerves were fraying, and he could see Mr. and Mrs. Bennet already hurrying from their room towards the congregated group. "SILENCE!" he shouted over Kitty's ranting.

"What is the meaning of this?" exclaimed Mr. Bennet.

No one had time to explain before Mrs. Bennet's fluttering and palpitations took over. "Dear lord, what happened here? I hope no one was hurt." Her eyes darted here and there, seeing broken glass all over the table, floor, and staircase. There was spilled water with loose flowers lying scattered on the floor. "Oh my, did someone break a vase? Well, I suppose it does not matter all that much. Mr. Darcy has enough money to buy another vase, I would wager he could purchase a hundred more if he wanted. It does not signify much anyway. From the look of it, it was an old, ugly thing. I would never allow such a vase in my home, especially in a place of prominence such as the top of the stairs where everyone can see it. Oh, and just look at the rug! It will be ruined if it is not tended to immediately."

Elizabeth was mortified by her mother for the second time that day, and it was only their second time in company. She dreaded the remainder of the holiday. It was almost a week before Christmas, and already she wished her mother had not come.

Fitzwilliam was already tired of Mrs. Bennet's ramblings. "Mrs. Bennet, I thank you for your concern about my rug. Perhaps it would be best that you accompany Elizabeth to the sitting room while I have Mrs. Reynolds clean this up." He motioned for Mrs. Reynolds to join them. She had taken a stance a few stairs below the top, out of the way of the family but close enough to be of service to Mr. and Mrs. Darcy when they needed her.

"Oh yes, Mr. Darcy, what a superb idea." She began to leave, but nearly stepped on a piece of glass. Fitzwilliam leapt to her side and offered his arm.

"Here, Mrs. Bennet let me help you. You almost stepped on a piece of broken vase. I fear you will cut your foot."

"Good Lord, did I truly almost cut it? Oh, that would have been terrible. I cannot imagine a cut foot at a time such as this. Why, in order to help you dear wife, I must be in the best of health. With a manor this size, with so many servants, I am sure she is quite overwhelmed. She will need me to help her decide what to serve and how best to entertain."

She continued rambling as Fitzwilliam led her down the stairs. Mr. Bennet, Mary, and Kitty followed, leaving Jane and Charles, who had just arrived, with Elizabeth and Mrs. Reynolds to decide what best to do.

"Jane, will you and Charles please go down and entertain Mother? Fitzwilliam will then be able to come back here and help us with this."

"Certainly, Lizzy, we will send him back straightaway." Jane and Charles rushed down the stairs, careful to avoid the shattered glass.

"Mrs. Reynolds, was this vase valuable?" Elizabeth asked as the two started to gather the scattered flowers and larger chunks that were easy to pick up without being cut.

"Valuable? Well, as a matter of strictly financial value, no, it was not. However, it does have a more sentimental value to the family."

Elizabeth's eyes were large with apprehension. She sucked in a deep breath and was just about to inquire further when Fitzwilliam returned.

"Mrs. Reynolds, that is not the vase I

think it is, is it?" His eyes were filled with concerned as he inquired.

"I am afraid so, Mr. Darcy."

Elizabeth was trembling as she heard her husband's words. Her eyes darted back and forth between them and the scattered pieces. "Why is this vase so important?" Elizabeth could barely ask her question, for she feared the answer.

Fitzwilliam took Elizabeth's hands in his and held them as he looked into her tear-filled eyes. "The vase was given to my mother, by my father, on the day of Georgiana's birth. It is always filled with my mother's favorite flowers."

"Orchids?" Elizabeth asked in a whisper as she held up a cut orchid that she had picked up off the floor.

Fitzwilliam did not say a word; he simply nodded his head. "The vase is special to Georgiana because our mother died shortly after her birth. She does not remember Mother, and she was still quite young when our father died almost six years ago. She has always felt this vase offered her a connection to our parents. We always keep it here, at the top of the stairs, where it can be admired by all that are welcomed into our family quarters."

Elizabeth was upset, distraught. "However will we tell her? Oh, Fitzwilliam, she will be devastated."

"We will figure something out, do not worry, Elizabeth. She is almost a grown woman, and although it will break her heart, she will get over it soon enough."

Mrs. Reynolds was already picking up the pieces and placing them into a basket. Her heart was breaking for her dear little Georgie. She agreed with Fitzwilliam that the girl's heart would be broken but, like him, was sure she would handle the situation with grace and poise. Mrs. Reynolds feared how she would suffer in the silence of her room, though; she was sure the tears would flow for hours.

The trio picked up chunks of the broken vase in silence, each lost in their own thoughts about what poor Georgiana would say when she found out. Finally, with the task completed, Mrs. Reynolds took care of the vase remnants and discarded flowers while Elizabeth and Fitzwilliam returned to their guests.

By the time Elizabeth and Fitzwilliam entered the sitting room to invite everyone to supper it was already a quarter past six. Elizabeth stood erect despite the pressure building in her head. She pressed her trembling palm to her cheek, trying to cool her flushed skin. Jane noticed Elizabeth's raised ire and approached her, gently touching her shoulder, offering support amongst the chaos of their family.

The room fell silent, and all eyes turned to Fitzwilliam and Elizabeth when the rest of the party realized they had entered the room.

The Bennets had only arrived three hours earlier, but already it felt as they had been here a week. *Do they actually plan to stay a fortnight?* Elizabeth was already beginning to dread the holidays that, until today, she had been looking forward to with such joy and anticipation. She was tempted to call off supper and send her parents and younger sisters to their rooms to pack. She was sure it was not too late to send them into Lambton to get rooms at the inn.

"I believe supper is ready. Shall we go in?" Elizabeth said in her *not to be questioned* voice.

Everyone stood to follow, but no one said a word. Though the vase had not been mentioned, everyone was sure it would soon be addressed. They were wrong; Fitzwilliam had no intention of bringing it up, and neither did Elizabeth.

The dining room was silent except for the shuffling of chairs against the floor. Even Mrs. Bennet held her tongue. Finally, jovial Charles could take it no more. "I say, Fitz, I remember there being more lively conversation at the table in the past. I know there was that recent business of the broken vase, but let me assure you the girls are terribly sorry and promise nothing like it will happen again. Am I right?" He looked first at Mary and then Kitty, and both girls vigorously nodded their heads in agreement. "Very good! I think it is all settled. Let us liven the place up a bit. I promise you will want to be in a good mood, for the Darcys have an amazing French cook you are all sure to love."

His invitation was all Mrs. Bennet needed. "A French cook! Why, I have never eaten food prepared by a French cook, but I have heard there are no better cooks in the world than French ones."

The tension in the room was palpable; it could almost be cut with a knife. Fitzwilliam confidently responded, "You are correct; our cook, Mrs. Lacroix, was born and raised in France. Both of her parents were chefs and she has been cooking from a young age. Cook studied French cuisine under some of the most renowned chefs in France. We were fortunate that Mrs. Lacroix came to Pemberley upon recommendation. She has since served our family with excellence these many years."

"She sounds incredible, Fitzwilliam. We are indeed grateful to be your guests here and experience her expertise," said Jane.

Charles smiled at his wife and reached out to squeeze her hand under the table. Both looked up as six servants entered carrying a variety of dishes. Each dish was placed upon the table and its cover removed. Everyone breathed deep; the aroma of fish, potatoes and gravy, sweet potatoes with a caramelized glaze, vegetables from the hot house, freshly baked bread with honey butter, and baked apples arrested their sense. A feast fit for a king.

Elizabeth was amazed at the quality and quantity of food Mrs. Lacroix was able to put together at such short notice. Supper seemed to be going off without a hitch, and Elizabeth began to relax and breathe easy. The servants returned to remove the empty dishes. All had been removed but one when the mayhem commenced. Mrs. Bennet pushed her chair away from the table at the same time a servant was reaching around to remove the final dish. Her chair hit him in the stomach and doubled him over, causing him to drop the dish onto the table in front of Mrs. Bennet. Her wine glass was toppled over, and the red liquid flowed freely over the table and onto the floor and Mrs. Bennet's finest slippers. "You clumsy fool, just look what you have done!"

Elizabeth's ire rose quickly. "Mother, you know as well as I whose fault it was, and it certainly was not his. Apologize this minute." She would not allow her mother to speak to the Pemberley staff in such an egregious manner.

"Apologize? To a servant? Never!" Mrs. Bennet was entirely out of line, and it was escalating. The servants were all scrambling to clean up the mess, except the one who had been hit with the chair. He had regained his composure and was standing near the wall looking at his shiny shoes. He feared he would lose his place over such a mishap. It would not be so terrible if it was not the first supper the new mistress had ever hosted at Pemberley.

"Now, Mother, I mean it. You will apologize this minute."

"I'm sorry, Lizzy."

"Not to me, to Jonathan."

Mrs. Bennet looked as if she were going to throw daggers at her daughter, but, with all the overly dramatic flourish she could muster, she made her apology. Jonathan accepted it, though he and everyone else in the room knew it was insincere. He was turning to make a hasty exit when Elizabeth addressed her mother again. "Now say it as if you mean it."

The room was silent. Jane and Charles, as well as Mary and Kitty, stared at their plates, trying to imagine the situation was not playing out as it was in front of them. Mr. Bennet was enjoying his second daughter scolding her mother, and Fitzwilliam could not be prouder that his wife was coming to the rescue of a servant even though it meant raising the ire of her mother. He knew how significant this was, considering how much

Elizabeth wished to avoid her mother's displeasure.

"Elizabeth Bennet Darcy, I have told the man I am sorry. I shall not say another word about it." Mrs. Bennet was livid at her daughter's insolence. Rarely did she use her daughters' full names, but when she did she meant business and was fully prepared to stand her ground. Mr. Bennet was concerned a battle would ensue, but his daughter handled the situation better than he imagined possible.

"Very well, Mother. I expect your trunks will be packed as soon as supper is finished. I imagine the inn at Lambton has sufficient room for the remainder of your stay." Mrs. Bennet opened her mouth to respond, but Elizabeth continued, not giving her a chance to argue. "This is my home, and my staff, and you will treat them with respect or you will not be allowed to remain."

Mrs. Bennet's eyes were piercing flames, but she held her tongue. Jane's eyes were full of fear and Charles clasped her hand under the table, offering as much support as he could. Mary and Kitty were amazed at Elizabeth's aplomb. They had never heard anyone speak to their mother in such a manner; though the five sisters had wanted to scold their mother in the past, no one had actually done it. Mr. Bennet leaned back in his chair with satisfaction. *Having my daughters married and under their own roofs is an uncommonly good strategy to put my wife in her place. Now, if Jane could pluck up her courage and do the same, the girls will turn out quite well,* he thought.

"The inn at Lambton ... well, I am not sure ... Mr. Bennet!" Mrs. Bennet was at a loss for words. Finally, Mr. Bennet came to her rescue.

"Well, Mrs. Bennet, I think you owe this lad an apology. Otherwise we will be removing to the inn. I must say, I would prefer the company of our family over an inn full of strangers after such a long journey, but if you cannot admit you were in the wrong, I suppose we must leave. Perhaps we could get the girls to attend you so that I might stay here at Pemberley, for it was not as if I offended the lad, and I have been so looking forward to spending some time in Mr. Darcy's library." He smiled at his wife and then addressed his two daughters. "What say you, Mary and Kitty? Would you prefer to avoid another episode with the vases of Pemberley and instead attend your mother in the village?"

Both girls sat in silence; their father had not actually meant to address them, and they knew it.

"Oh, Mr. Bennet, of course I do not want to be sent away. You of all people should know how clumsy I am, and when it happens I lose my mind with worry and distress. Of course it is my fault, I just needed a few minutes to calm my nerves and see the situation clearly. Young man, come here!" She waved her hand around, beckoning Jonathan to come near her. "You know I did not mean to blame this episode on you. I fear I am a clumsy woman and just did not realize what happened. I am sorry. Please accept my apology."

Jonathan nodded to Mrs. Bennet, unsure if he should say anything. The tension in the room was intense, and he simply wanted to be away. It seemed as if his nod was sufficient, and Mrs. Darcy dismissed him and the other servants, asking them to advise Mrs. Reynolds that they would take their dessert in the sitting room. Once they were gone, she gave her mother a final scolding. "I am mightily glad you chose to apologize, Mother, for I much prefer you remain at

Pemberley, but please remember I will not hesitate to send you away if you mistreat even one member of the Pemberley staff. I have been mistress here only a short time, and I will not allow you to come in and stir up trouble before I have gained the staff's trust and loyalty. Am I understood?"

Mrs. Bennet nodded, afraid to say anything for fear it would be wrong.

"Very well. Let us all go to the sitting room for dessert."

The entire party stood and followed Fitzwilliam and Elizabeth to the sitting room. Once the dining room was vacated, the staff returned to clean up. There was much chatter about the new mistress, and had they wondered how the new Mrs. Darcy would treat them, they had their answer. It took less than an hour for the whole of the estate to hear the entire story. That night Elizabeth had gained the respect of the staff and the unwavering support of the servant she had demanded justice for.

## Chapter 5

"Oh, my mother drives me absolutely insane," Elizabeth huffed as she and Fitzwilliam retired for the night.

"She does have a way of trying one's patience," Fitzwilliam responded. He was sitting on the chair near the window, removing his boots and watching Elizabeth pace the full length of the room. "Elizabeth, if you do not stop pacing you will ruin the rug."

She paused and looked at the rug, half expecting to see it disintegrate under her gaze. When she saw it was intact, she began pacing again, hardly recognizing Fitzwilliam's jest. "The nerve of my mother, coming here to our house and acting as if she owns the place. Why, I have only been here a short time, and much of it has been spent here in this room. How are the staff to know

I am not like my mother? I wish she had never come." Fitzwilliam listened to her rant while she continued to pace. "Poor Jane, she is too sweet and kind to tell mother to stop interfering, and now she hardly feels her house is her own. Mother continually shows up and changes everything Jane does. Why ... why ...," Elizabeth was so upset she could barely complete her sentence, "why, I would banish her from my house!"

"Banish her! Now, Elizabeth, do not you think that is a little harsh?"

"No, I do not. Were you not there at supper? Did you not see how she treated Jonathan? It will not be allowed here, and I will talk to Jane tomorrow. We will put Mother in her place so Jane and Charles have some peace at Netherfield until they relocate to the north."

"Relocate to the north? What are you talking about?"

Elizabeth paused in her pacing, "Oh dear, I cannot believe I forgot to tell you. So much has happened today that it slipped my mind. Yes, Jane and Charles are giving up Netherfield and leasing an estate but seven miles from here. Is it not splendid news?"

"Yes it is. I will speak to Charles about it tomorrow."

"Just remember it is still a secret; only we are to know."

"Do not worry, I will not tell a soul. Now, about your mother and her interference with your sister. You will do nothing. Jane and Charles are not you and me; they prefer to handle things differently. You will stay out of their business. Promise me!"

Before answering, she walked to the edge of the bed and flopped down with a little pout. "Very well, I promise not to get involved. If Jane asks me I will assist her, but I promise not to approach her about it." Elizabeth perked up a little as she continued, "I am glad for my sake, though now that I know they are planning to move nearby next summer I am absolutely desperate for time to pass. I dearly want my sister near. My family, on the other hand, may all move to America for all I care."

Fitzwilliam chuckled at his wife's dramatics. "You do not mean that. You would miss them if they went to America." His boots and clothing were removed down to his trousers and linen shirt, which was open at his neck. He walked to Elizabeth's side then, scooping her into his arms, he took her place on the bed and sat her in his lap. Wrapping his arms around her, he nuzzled her neck right below her cheek. "I know you too well. Your mother may irritate you, but if some ungentlemanlike man condescended to slight her, or any other member of your family, he would be sent on his way with a rather scathing scolding."

His words made her smile, and she chose to tease him a little in return. "Oh, you think you know me so well, do you? Well, you are correct, and if said ungentlemanlike man were to apologize properly, he, like my mother, would be admitted back into my good graces. If not, he too would be cast off like an old slipper, lost and forgotten, never thought of again." Elizabeth flipped her slipper off her foot, sending it spiraling through the air to land near Fitzwilliam's boots.

"Oh, really, just like that, you would throw him away."

"Yes, just like that."

Reaching up with both hands on either side of her face, he turned her so he could gaze into her eyes. "I am glad I am no longer ungentlemanlike and that I was able to apologize, for I never want to be cast from your good graces. I love you too much."

"Even with such a mother?"

He remained steadfast and serious in his response. "Yes, even with such a mother. I have grown to appreciate your mother."

"Appreciate her? Never!"

"Yes, I appreciate her. For she raised you, and I love you."

"Well, when you put it that way." Elizabeth melted into Fitzwilliam's arms, enjoying the strength of his embrace. Finally, she was able to sit up and forget the evening and move on. "Will you unbutton my gown? I intend to get out of this thing. It is lovely, but I had entirely forgotten how stiff it is. I feel as if I am wearing a bone corset. Oh, how I hate corsets."

Elizabeth leaned her head forward, giving him full access to the buttons down the back of her gown, which he undid, and then allowed his hands to linger on her back, rubbing and massaging away her stress.

"Be careful, if you begin I may never let you cease. You have no idea the knots my mother causes in my neck and back." Elizabeth meant what she said, but she also wanted to remove the dress. She slipped from his lap and stepped out of her gown, throwing it over the back of the chair where Fitzwilliam had left his jacket, vest, and cravat. The chair was quickly becoming their favorite place to discard the evening's clothing until Mr. Carson and Gracie put them in their proper place.

Walking to the washbasin to splash water on her face, Elizabeth stood erect. Turning to Fitzwilliam, who was turning down their bed, she exclaimed, "Fitzwilliam, we were meant to decorate the tree tonight. I wanted it to be a surprise, just the two of us, but I entirely forgot. It is already set up in the drawing room. The decorations have been gathered and are in a wooden box nearby. Oh, what a disaster. I wanted it to be decorated for when Georgiana returns tomorrow. Do you think we will have time to decorate it in the morning?"

"Yes, I am sure we will."

"Oh, but my family will be around. I had something special planned." Elizabeth's bottom lip stuck out in a little pout Fitzwilliam adored. He stepped to her side and took her hands in his.

"Come, let us go do it now. Everyone has

retired to their rooms; it will just be the two of us."

Her eyes lit up at the prospect, but then dimmed, "No, let's just stay here. I do not want to get dressed again. It can wait until tomorrow."

"There is no need for you to get dressed. Just slip on your dressing gown and let us go down."

Elizabeth looked at her husband, his eyes bright with the prospect of her *something special*, and then towards her robe that lay on the seat of her vanity. She supposed he was correct. They could go down, and no one would ever know. She released his hands and reached for her robe, which Fitzwilliam helped slip over her shoulders. Elizabeth wrapped it around her and tied it snug at her waist. The two left the room and walked to the drawing room, the light from the small candle Fitzwilliam carried lighting their way.

When they entered the drawing room, Elizabeth rushed to the box of decorations at the far side of the room. It was just as she had left it, and Mrs. Reynolds had done her part despite the interruptions they had experienced. Wrapping her hands around the two mugs to ensure they were still warm, Elizabeth turned back to Fitzwilliam. "It is not as hot as it once was, but it is still plenty warm." Elizabeth handed him a mug, keeping the other for herself. "Mrs. Reynolds tells me caramel hot chocolate is one of your favorite holiday treats. I thought we could enjoy a mug while we decorate the tree."

A wide smile erupted on Fitzwilliam's face as he took the mug from his wife. She watched as he breathed in the rich scent and then took a large swallow. "Mmm, this is divine, just how I like it." He took another drink, remembering all of the reasons why he enjoyed it so well. He sat his mug on the table then reached for Elizabeth's and sat it beside his. He gathered her in an embrace, and she tasted the delicacy for the first time when she licked the residue off his lips.

The two took their time sharing their drinks and decorating the tree. It was well past midnight when their laughter was heard by another who was still up. Mr. Bennet had seen his wife to their room and, once she was asleep, he had crept downstairs to find the library. He had spent close to an hour searching the shelves, selecting book after book to enjoy during his stay. He had just stepped from the room and closed the door when he heard talking and saw light coming from the drawing room. Sneaking over, he peeked through the doorway and watched his daughter and son-in-law putting the finishing touches on their Christmas tree.

"I think it is a splendid tree. What think you, Elizabeth?" Fitzwilliam said as he placed the last ornament as high as he could reach.

Walking to his side, she wrapped her arm around his waist and responded, "I think it is more beautiful than any tree ever seen. I am sure everyone will love it when they see it tomorrow." She stretched up on her tip-toes and kissed him upon the cheek, but that was not enough for him. He scooped her into his arms and playfully dipped her, kissing her as he held her suspended above the floor.

Elizabeth clasped her hands tight to his forearms and giggled. "Fitzwilliam, what do you think you are doing?"

"Nothing," he stated as he kissed her again, still not raising her to her feet.

"Nothing! Why, this is unquestionably something!" Elizabeth giggled again as he lifted her to her feet and then swept her into his arms. Carrying her to the couch, he sat down with her still in his arms, kissing her deeply. Elizabeth sighed against him. As their passions increased she hitched up her robe and turned to straddle him. His hands settled on each of her hips as she leaned forward and commanded a response from his lips.

Mr. Bennet had seen enough. He turned to leave as his daughter's hands search her husband's body. He was halfway up the stairs when he heard Fitzwilliam's distinct groan, "Oh, God, Elizabeth, do that again." He rushed to his room and shut the door, unable to witness his child in the throes of passion with her new husband.

## Chapter 6

Elizabeth endured a restless night, and when she woke the following morning she felt as if she had not slept at all. Today Georgiana and Colonel Fitzwilliam were to arrive, and she was to play hostess to the entire party. She had been working endlessly with Mrs. Reynolds to prepare the manor for her guests, and in her opinion it was lovely. Everything had been falling perfectly into place until her family had shown up uninvited. Now, rather than relax and enjoy a carefree holiday, Elizabeth waited in anticipation for the next catastrophe to ensue, for she knew there was bound to be more. How could there not be with her family in residence?

Fitzwilliam, on the other hand, had had the responsibility of running a large estate and the problems that often occur with such authority for so long that he rarely slept poorly. He woke when he felt his wife stirring in the bed beside him. Rolling over, he wrapped an arm around her and pulled her close. He could feel the tension in her body.

"Elizabeth, what is the matter? Did you not sleep well?"

"No, I did not. Having my family come has disturbed my tranquility. I am happy to see Jane again, but having Mamma here has already put me on edge, and she has not even been here twenty-four hours. She plans on staying almost two full weeks! What am I to do?" Elizabeth let out an exasperated breath then slipped out from under Fitzwilliam's arm to arise from bed.

"Elizabeth, it is terribly early. There is no need to rise so soon. Here, come back to bed." Fitzwilliam flipped down the bed covers and patted the bed next to him as he spoke to her.

"No, I cannot. I must help Mrs. Reynolds prepare for the arrival of your sister and cousin."

"Mrs. Reynolds can handle the preparations. She is highly skilled at her job." Fitzwilliam raised an eyebrow questioningly as he continued, "Do you doubt the proficiency of the Pemberley staff?"

Though he teased, he did not diminish her anxiety.

"You know I do not doubt Mrs. Reynolds, nor the rest of the Pemberley staff. It is just that most of your staff have never seen the likes of my mother."

"Well, if you will not join me then I will join you." Fitzwilliam began to stand.

"No, no, you rest. We were up late last night, and there is no point in both of us going without sleep."

Her argument was futile. Fitzwilliam had already gotten out of bed to begin his day. Just as Elizabeth tied the sash of her dressing gown at her slender waist, she felt his strong arms wrap around her, and he pressed his lips to the soft skin right below her ear. Elizabeth leaned her head to the side, providing him greater access. Accepting her invitation, he increased the attentions of his mouth while allowing his hands to roam and massage her shoulders and back.

Elizabeth was tense, but he could feel her muscles relax beneath his loving ministrations.

"Come, let us dress and go downstairs. It will not be long before my family stirs, and I do not want them roaming Pemberley alone," Elizabeth said when his hands stilled.

"They will not be alone. Mrs. Reynolds will make sure they are taken care of."

"You know what I mean. I need to be around to keep my mother in check. There is no telling what she is apt to say." Elizabeth unwrapped Fitzwilliam's arms and dressed with a little more energy than she had begun with. Fitzwilliam had to rush, but he was ready in enough time to attend her to the breakfast parlour.

Only Mr. Bennet was there when Fitzwilliam and Elizabeth entered the breakfast parlour together. He was sitting at the far end of the table with a few books laid out in front of him while he sipped a cup of tea.

"Good morning, Father," Elizabeth said as she walked to his side and offered him a kiss on the cheek.

Mr. Bennet smiled at the simple act. Until he received her kiss, he had not realized how much he had missed it the past few weeks since her marriage and subsequent relocation to the north. "Good morning, my dear. How are you?"

"I am well. I see you must have found Fitzwilliam's library. Did you sleep at all last night, or were you too occupied with books?"

"Ah, yes, a place I could easily lose myself in for months—years, perhaps. It is an impressive library, sir. I have never seen its equal in a private collection. You should be proud. I did sleep a little, but not as much as an old man such as myself should."

Elizabeth turned her loving eyes to the face of Fitzwilliam. He stood tall with his shoulders squared. It was the stance of a man who had hundreds of families dependent upon him; the stance of a man who knew who he was and what he wanted from life; the stance of a man with confidence and superior breeding. A stance Elizabeth was learning to love.

Fitzwilliam held Elizabeth's chair for her as she sat down. He then took the seat next to her and addressed Mr. Bennet. "Thank you, sir. It has been the work of many generations. I have added a lot to the library, as did my father before me. In days such as these, when great books are so readily available, it would be neglectful of me not to add to it regularly."

"I quite see your meaning, sir. I have a

modest library at Longbourn, considering the size of my estate, but it is nothing to the one you have here."

Elizabeth reached for a dish of eggs, piling a bit first on Fitzwilliam's plate and then her own. She continued the process until both of their plates were heaped with eggs, shredded potatoes, sausage, and toast with melted butter and preserves. She then prepared her husband a cup of tea and was just preparing her own when her father addressed her. "Well, Lizzy, you must be hungry this morning." He pointed at the plates she had prepared.

"Yes, we stayed up rather late last night completing some tasks we were unable to finish due to your unexpected arrival," Elizabeth responded.

"Ah, yes, the tree decorations. I looked in the drawing room this morning and saw someone had been busy last night."

"What do you think of it?"

"I thought it very pretty. In fact, I think your entire house looks extremely pretty indeed. I can see you have taken considerable pride in running your own home." He pointed at the centerpiece on the table and the matching one on the sideboard.

"Thank you, Father. You are right, I have enjoyed preparing Pemberley for the holidays. I know Mamma does not believe I—"

"Pish-posh, forget what your mother thinks for once and care only what the two of you think."

Elizabeth looked at her father, a little shocked. Never had he told her to ignore her mother's feelings and care only for her own. She considered this must be what it was like to be *all grown up*. She was just about to respond to him when there was a slight tap at the door. It opened to reveal Mrs. Reynolds.

"Mr. Darcy, sir, this express just arrived from Miss Darcy." She held out the missive and Fitzwilliam took it from her hands.

"Thank you, I will read it directly." He looked at Elizabeth and Mr. Bennet as he opened the letter. "Pray excuse me a moment while I read what she has to say."

Elizabeth watched her husband's expression fall slightly as he progressed through the note, then handing it to her, he allowed her to read it. Elizabeth read the missive with eyes wide with panic.

*My Dear Brother,*

*I hope you and my new sister,*

*Elizabeth, are well. I am very excited to join the both of you at Pemberley later this week.*

*Please do not be angry, but Aunt Matlock has been hinting she should be invited to Pemberley for Christmas. I am sorry, brother, but her hints were so obvious that I would have to be a fool not to understand them. Aunt Matlock was beginning to lose patience with me not extending the invitation, so I did.*

*I fear I must warn you that not only will Richard and I arrive on Friday, but Lord and Lady Matlock, as well as cousin James and his wife, Roslynd, and their three children, will also arrive with us.*

*I must apologize to you and Elizabeth, but, brother, I knew not what else to do. I do not want them cross with me.*

*Your Loving Sister,*

*Georgiana*

Elizabeth's skin went pale as she looked at Fitzwilliam and exclaimed, "I do not believe it! Is she serious? Seven more are to be added to our party! If you will excuse me, I must speak to Mrs. Reynolds and Mrs. Lacroix immediately." Elizabeth did, in actuality, believe what Georgiana had written, though listening to her outburst one would think she did not. She stood up, but her legs were too weak to take her to the door. Fitzwilliam noticed and beckoned her to sit.

"I will ring the bell for Mrs. Reynolds. Let her come to you. The rest of the family are not up yet and it is likely they will not be for another hour."

Elizabeth fell back into her seat while Fitzwilliam rang the bell for Mrs. Reynolds. Mr. Bennet eyed Elizabeth, a little concerned by her pale features. He dared not ask who the additional seven guests were, but he need not wonder long, for it was only a minute or two before the door opened to admit the housekeeper. "Sir, madame, you called?" Mrs. Reynolds inquired.

"Yes," Elizabeth said as she patted the table next to her. "Please come here so I may speak with you."

Mrs. Reynolds sat next to Elizabeth. "How may I help you, Mrs. Darcy?"

Elizabeth laid the letter on the table in front of her and clasped her hands over the top of it. "The express that recently arrived was from Miss Darcy, and informed us that an additional seven members of the Fitzwilliam family will be arriving with her and the Colonel. It seems that the Earl and Lady Matlock, as well as their eldest son and his wife, Lord and Lady James Fitzwilliam, and their three young children will be arriving today. Our original holiday party of six is now a crowd of seventeen." Elizabeth put a trembling hand upon the arm of Mrs. Reynolds. "Do you think we can accommodate so many people?"

"Yes, Mrs. Darcy, you need not fear. I will send Abigail and Elspeth to prepare some more rooms. I will also inform Mrs. Lacroix of the extra guests and have her revise the menu accordingly. Do you want to change the menu, or just increase the portions?"

Elizabeth looked to her husband. "Do you have any special requests for the meals while your relations are in residence, or shall we proceed with my original menu?"

"Your menu will be perfect, my dear.

There is no need to change it." Fitzwilliam was cross with his Uncle and Aunt, as well as his cousin's family. Why now, of all times, would they barge in? They had rarely been to Pemberley since the death of his mother almost fifteen years prior. He was upset that they chose now, his and Elizabeth's first Christmas as husband and wife, to come. It was one thing to be invited, but another entirely to invite oneself. There was entirely too much self-invitation happening this holiday season.

Elizabeth was relieved. She had neither the time nor the energy to prepare another menu. This one had taken her a full two days to get just the right combination of everyone's favourite dishes. She hoped their new guests would have similar tastes as those she originally planned the menu around. "Mrs. Reynolds, there is one last thing we need to discuss." Elizabeth looked at her father out of the corner of her eye. He was not likely to say anything, but she was sure he would see the wisdom in her final instruction.

"What is it, Mrs. Darcy?"

"At no time is my mother to sit next to the Earl and Lady Matlock or Lord and Lady

Fitzwilliam. She is to sit near me or my sister Jane so that we may keep her in check."

Mrs. Reynolds acknowledged Elizabeth's request with a nod, noticing the smirk upon Mr. Bennet's face. He clearly understood why his daughter was making the request.

Mrs. Reynolds had only just left the room to have bedrooms prepared and Mrs. Lacroix informed of the additions when the rest of the family joined the Darcys and Mr. Bennet for breakfast.

"I hope you all slept well, for Elizabeth and I have an announcement to make," Fitzwilliam said after everyone had been seated and dished their plates. "Just this morning an express came from my sister, Georgiana. It seems our family party will not only be blessed with our Bennet relations, but we have just received the happy news that we will have an additional seven guests from our Fitzwilliam relations. They will be arriving this evening before supper. I hope you do not mind sharing your holiday with a rather large crowd, for it appears that by the end of the day there will be seventeen of us celebrating the Christmas holiday together."

"Seventeen," exclaimed Mrs. Bennet. "So many! Elizabeth, it is a fine thing I arrived when I did, for you would never be able to host such a number."

"Mother, I promise you I already have it well under control. Rooms are being prepared as we speak, and Cook has already been instructed about the menu. I thank you for your offer, but your are on holiday. Please, go enjoy yourself; there is no need to fret over my household."

"But, Lizzy, are you sure? I have so much more experience than you at hosting lavish parties. Why, look at the splendid job I did hosting yours and Jane's double wedding. I have recently had such good practice that I am sure my assistance will be invaluable."

"Thank you, Mother, but no. I must learn to manage these things myself."

Fitzwilliam squeezed Elizabeth's knee under the table, proud of how easily she was handling a difficult situation.

"Very well, Lizzy, but when everything falls apart you will have no one but yourself to blame. Do not come running to me later if you will not accept my help now."

Mrs. Bennet turned her attention to Fitzwilliam as if she had not been scolding his wife seconds before. "Fitzwilliam, the room you gave us is wonderful. I do not think

I have slept that well on a bed other than my own since before I was married."

"I am glad you approve of it, Mrs. Bennet. Elizabeth picked the room especially for you." It was a half-truth, for had Elizabeth received more advanced notice that they were coming, Mrs. Reynolds would have advised her to put her parents in that room.

"I am sure with only a few weeks to get to know the manor, and such a large manor it is, that it is unlikely she would have known the best rooms to offer her guests. I am sure we only received the room because of your vast knowledge of the estate."

Jane was mortified that their mother was belittling every action Elizabeth performed in her own home. It was the exact thing she had been doing at Netherfield for the past three weeks. She was proud of Elizabeth for standing up for herself and wished she had the courage to do the same.

# Chapter 7

Elizabeth was surprised how fast the time of their guests' arrival crept up on her. It seemed she had just gotten up from breakfast when Mrs. Reynolds sought her out to inform her that the Matlock and Fitzwilliam carriages were spotted coming up the drive. Just yesterday she had stood at the same window watching the progress of their guests, and now she was doing it again, and with just as much trepidation.

"Elizabeth, my dear, they are here," Fitzwilliam said as he entered the room and stood watching her with concern. She had not been her lively self today, but rather was prone to silence and deep contemplation. He had asked her, when they had a moment alone, if everything was all right, but, as women do, she assured him she was fine and put on a charming smile with all pretense of happiness. He had come to know her well the past months and knew it was a show to put him at ease while she fretted in silence.

"I have been watching their progress." For a moment, Elizabeth let her guard down. "Do you think everything will be well, or shall we end up with as many disasters as we have already had? To think, we have had these complications with only half the family in residence." The nervousness upon her countenance was clear, and Fitzwilliam wrapped his arms around her for comfort.

"Fear not, all the mishaps are sure to be over. We haven't many relations left to descend upon us, unless, of course, Aunt Catherine decides to grace us with her presence."

Elizabeth swatted him in a gentle scolding. "Do not even think such things. If she arrives, you will have to admit me to an asylum, for surely I would lose my good sense and go insane." Her anxiety drove her desperate desire to taste his lips again. She turned in his arms, and despite the fact that her rational mind was screaming that their guests were eminent, she sought his lips for a sustaining kiss. It was not until she heard the butler open the door that she pulled away from him, reached for his hand, and led him towards the front door. Their sudden yet passionate contact had not been much, but it was enough to whet his need for her. Fitzwilliam silently cursed the arrival of so many guests, and wished they could return to the solitude of their rooms that their first few weeks of marriage had afforded them.

As soon as they stepped into the hallway, Georgiana rushed to her brother and threw her arms around him. "I am so sorry, Fitzwilliam. I did not know how not to invite them. They were pressuring me so much. Please do not scold me."

"Fear not, Georgie, we are not upset with you."

"What a relief, brother! I have been on nerves these past two days complete."

Colonel Richard Fitzwilliam and the Earl and Lady Matlock entered the house in a more refined manner than Georgiana had. "Fitzwilliam," Lady Matlock cooed as she approached him, engulfing him in a motherly hug that he always enjoyed. In the years since his own mother's death, she had been a surrogate mother of sorts to him and Georgiana. "I am so glad Georgiana invited us to spend the Christmas holiday here at

Pemberley. It has been far too long since we were here. Why, I think the last time we were here at Christmastime was before your poor mother left us, God rest her soul."

"Welcome, Aunt. We are pleased you could come," Fitzwilliam said. Upon his statement, the door opened again to receive Lord and Lady James Fitzwilliam and their three lively children.

"Grandmother!" the children shouted and ran to the Countess, who knelt down and swept all three of them into an engulfing hug.

"Hello, my dears, how was your trip?"

Three little voices were heard exclaiming about how cold and uncomfortable it was in the carriage. Finally, little James's voice was heard above the rest. "Mamma said we could not ride in your carriage on the way here because Uncle Richard and Georgie were riding with you, but she promised us that if you said yes, we could ride home with you. Can we? Can we return to Matlock with you and Grandfather when it is time to go home?" Lady Matlock looked at her daughter-in-law as Roslynd shrugged her shoulders.

"We will see, little ones. I think it

will depend on how well you behave at Pemberley."

"Oh, we will be good, for Mamma and Papa have said they will take all our presents away if we are not."

Elizabeth and Fitzwilliam smiled at the innocence of the children ruining all their parents hard laid plans to appear as if they had well-behaved offspring.

"Welcome, Lord and Lady Matlock, Lord and Lady Fitzwilliam. We are so pleased to have you here." Elizabeth stepped forward. "Will you not come in and get warm?"

"Thank you, my dear, but it is just James and Lillian, or Uncle and Aunt, if you prefer. There is no need to act upon ceremony when it is just us." Lady Matlock wrapped her arms around Elizabeth in a familial hug, something Elizabeth had not expected.

"Thank you, Aunt Lillian."

Lord and Lady Fitzwilliam stepped forward with their children and offered the same. "James and Roslynd will do for us," James said, and then leaned in a little conspiratorially and further stated, "though if you are upset, I will let my father respond to James and I will just assume I did not hear you." Then, as if he had not said anything amiss, he swept his three children in front of him and prattled off their introductions. "This upstanding young man is James III. Then we have our daughter, Evelyn, and our youngest son, Richard." James, Evelyn, and little Richard bowed and curtsied before Elizabeth.

She knelt in front of them and inquired further about their journey. "Did you have a good trip?"

"Um-hmm." Three little heads bobbed in front of her.

"I heard you say it was cold. Was it almost unbearable?"

"Oh yes, very cold. Little Richard got to sit on Mama's lap when his fingers were too cold. I would have liked to warm up on Mama's lap too, but she says I am getting too big," stated Evelyn in a matter-of-fact voice.

"Do you think some hot chocolate will help to warm your fingers and toes?" Elizabeth looked to Roslynd for her agreement. She nodded.

The three children's eyes lit up. "Yes, I think that would help us warm up a great deal."

"Very well, you three come with me while your mamma and papa go to their rooms to freshen up." Three little hands reached for her as she led them off to the kitchen, calling over her shoulder, "I will take these three with me. Fitzwilliam will make sure you all get to your rooms." She paused as she remembered one last thing. Turning towards all of them, she said, "We are extremely pleased you have all come to Pemberley for Christmas. I should tell you we had four other unexpected guests arrive just yesterday. In addition to my sister Jane and her husband arriving from Hertfordshire, my father, mother, and two younger sisters also arrived. You all should be aware that we will have a lively group of seventeen here for Christmas." Elizabeth left their shocked faces to Fitzwilliam as she gathered up her three charges and led them on their quest for hot chocolate.

Georgiana was the most surprised. "Seventeen! What an increase from our expected six. Is it true, though, that Mary and Kitty are here?"

"Yes, they are in their rooms at present. Elizabeth asked to greet you without the confusion of so many."

"Oh, what fun! I cannot wait to see them

again. They are as dear to me as Elizabeth. May I go and see them at once?"

"Yes, I am sure they would enjoy that." Georgiana began to hasten towards the stairs as her brother called out to her. "Georgie, we are very glad you are home, dearest." Georgiana ran back to her brother and gave him one last hug.

"As am I, brother."

As she released her arms from his neck and turned back to the stairs, Fitzwilliam said, "Once you have visited with Mary and Kitty and had a chance to get settled, I would speak with you."

"Very well, brother, I will come to you later." Then she ran up the stairs in search of the Bennet sisters.

The three Fitzwilliam children were adorable as Elizabeth set them down in the kitchen with their mugs of hot chocolate and talked with them. It was staggering what could be learned from three young children who liked to talk about everything their parents said, despite the fact that their parents would most assuredly prefer their conversations left unrepeated.

"Mrs. Darcy, are you angry that we came without being invited?"

"No, James, of course not. Why would you ask such a thing?"

"Because I overheard Grandmamma and Mamma talking, and they said that all of us coming without being invited by you directly is a *great impropriety*. They said that they should not *impose upon a newly married couple so suddenly*." James was pleased he was able to recite his mother's statements as precisely as he had.

"Mrs. Darcy, what does impropriety mean?" he asked innocently.

"Children, we are family now. You may call me Lizzy if you want."

The children looked at Elizabeth excitedly, and little Evelyn energetically responded, "I love the name Lizzy. I wanted to call you by it when I heard your sister call you Lizzy at your wedding, but Mamma said I could not until you invited me to. I am so glad you did. Do you want to know what?" Evelyn was bouncing as she spoke.

"What?" Elizabeth asked.

"I named my doll Lizzy, after you. She has the same dark brown hair you have. Her name used to be Mandoline, but I changed it after you married Cousin Fitzwilliam. I like the name Lizzy much better."

"What a pretty thing to say! Thank you, Evelyn. I am honoured."

"Lizzy, you did not answer my question," James protested over his sisters excitement.

"Oh yes, impropriety. Well, the best way to describe it is to do something improper."

Evelyn spoke up with panic, "Improper! Mamma says we should never do anything improper. That is very bad!"

All three of the Fitzwilliam children became sullen in their expression, afraid they had done something wrong.

"It is only wrong if the other person thinks it is wrong, I am so happy you are here that it could never be wrong or improper."

Suddenly their faces lit up with broad smiles. "Oh, good, because we want to be here. Are we going to have Christmas pudding?" asked James.

Little Richard looked up with hopeful eyes, his mug of chocolate oversized in his little hands.

"I had not thought about Christmas pudding. Do you like it?"

"Oh yes, we must have Christmas pudding. Grandfather says no Christmas is complete without it, and he would be cross the entire year if he did not eat it at Christmas dinner."

"He would! Well, we cannot have a cross grandfather, now can we? Christmas pudding it is." Turning towards Cook, who stood at the cookpot on the other side of the kitchen, she asked, "Mrs. Lacroix, did you hear that?"

"I certainly did, Madame. Christmas pudding is decidedly on the menu."

Elizabeth nodded her thanks and redirected her attention back to the children. "Is there anything else that you, your parents, or grandparents want to eat at Christmas dinner?"

"Um ..." Now that they were put on the spot, their little minds could not think of a single thing; instead they drank down their chocolate and asked for more.

"No, I think I should take you back to your parents. We will have more hot chocolate tomorrow."

"Promise?" the three called in unison.

"I promise."

Elizabeth gathered the children and took them to the suite of rooms they would share with their parents. As soon as they entered, all three dropped Elizabeth's hands and rushed to their mother. With excited voices, they exclaimed, "Mamma, Lizzy said we could call her Lizzy. And we get hot chocolate tomorrow, too. She also said she is going to have Christmas pudding at dinner. Now Grandfather does not have to be cross all year. Also, us coming is not improper because she wants us here." Their enthusiasm would have been contagious had not Roslynd's distress been heightened with every word they were saying. James and Roslynd looked towards the door where Elizabeth stood. Roslynd's face was pale and she was nervously glancing between her husband and Elizabeth, unsure if she should start apologizing right away or not.

"You are correct, children. Christmas pudding will certainly be served, and I dare you to get Cousin Fitzwilliam to miss even one day of hot chocolate. As far as being invited to Pemberley, we are family; you may come anytime you like. Whether it is with a month's notice or without a moment's notice, you will always be welcome here."

Roslynd's relief was palpable, and she smiled at Elizabeth. "Thank you, you have set my mind at ease. We worried about barging in, but we could not resist when James and

Lillian said they were coming. We knew Richard would be here too. It is common for us to spend the holiday together. We could not help but follow them here."

"Do not worry, you are most welcome. Now, if you will forgive me, I want to make sure everyone else is settled. I will see you at supper."

Elizabeth sought out her husband, who was still with the Matlocks in their rooms. She welcomed them as she had the Fitzwilliams, assured them their coming was actually a blessing to all, insisted she was glad they had come, and had just invited them to supper when her mother was heard in the hall.

"Lizzy, there you are, my dear. Have all of your guests arrived? When do we get to see them again?"

"You will see them at supper. For now, they are resting," Elizabeth said as she left Fitzwilliam at the Matlocks' door and met her mother down the hall.

"La, Lizzy, there is no need to stand upon ceremony and wait until supper. We are practically family! We may as well become better acquainted now." Mrs. Bennet continued to walk towards the Matlocks' rooms. She was undeterred by Elizabeth's repeated requests to allow them to rest.

Lady Matlock and Mrs. Bennet had met at the Darcys' wedding, and although they did not have a chance to get to know one another well, they were polite enough in one another's company. Lady Matlock heard Mrs. Bennet in the hall and stepped out to greet her. "Mrs. Bennet, I am so happy to see you again."

"And I you," Mrs. Bennet cooed, excited that a lady of rank was addressing her with such familiarity. "I had no inkling we would be spending Christmas together. Why, what a blessing this is indeed. I was just telling Mr. Bennet how excited I was when I heard you were coming. With both of us here, we will be able to ensure my Lizzy is able to handle her first Christmas in her new position of responsibility with remarkably little trouble. Pemberley is so much larger than Longbourn; I fear she will be out of her element."

"Mama," Lizzy scolded her mother in a terse whisper.

"Oh, Lizzy, there is no need to scold me. No one here is going to judge how you keep house, for we all know you are still learning.

What with your education taking place at as simple a country estate as Longbourn, no one will fault you for not knowing what is required of you in such a vast estate as Pemberley. That is why it will be agreeable to have us more experience ladies here to help you." Mrs. Bennet was nodding towards Lady Matlock the whole time as if she knew what was required of managing such a large estate.

"I thank you for your kind offer, but I hope both of you will simply enjoy your time at Pemberley and leave the household matters to me. Mrs. Reynolds has been managing Pemberley for many years in the absence of a mistress, and she is very well able to help me with whatever is required. As much as I appreciate your kind offer to help, I will not need it. Now, if you will excuse me, I must perform some of those duties you have so kindly brought to my attention. I will see you at supper."

Lady Matlock was already calculating how interesting this holiday would be with such an outspoken woman in their midst, and if she would admit it, she felt a little guilty that she was there for the same purpose as the brash Mrs. Bennet, though she would never have been so bold as to mention her motives aloud, and in front of the lady. A little regret regarding her actions crossed her mind, but she just as quickly pushed it away. She had been surprised when Elizabeth spoke up in her own defense, and not a little impressed.

Elizabeth left the group staring at her back as she rushed off to perform her duties, thankful to leave their criticisms behind, but a little guilty that she had left Fitzwilliam to separate her mother and Lady Matlock.

# Chapter 8

The whole party had assembled in the drawing room and was ready to enter the dining room for supper. Elizabeth's gaze swept over the group, falling upon her newest sister, Georgiana. Her heart ached for the young girl who had wept genuine tears of sorrow when her brother had told her about her mother's vase. Elizabeth had feared she would not soon recover, but seeing her now, well on her way to mending, relieved much of Elizabeth's distress. Mary and Kitty knew Georgiana had been told of their part in the event and made it their duty to provide solace to her troubled soul. Ultimately, Georgiana was too happy to have them with her at Pemberley to wallow in sorrow and self-pity.

Elizabeth's eyes continued around the room. She was apprehensive when so many sets stared back at her. Her mind raced at how her little holiday party of six had grown to such monumental proportions. She reached for Fitzwilliam and linked her arm through his, a clear indication it was time to go in. He understood and made the announcement for the company to follow him as he led the way to the dining room. Everyone followed in the proper order of rank as propriety demanded, excepting the Fitzwilliam children who ran hither and thither, weaving between the legs of their parents, grandparents, and everyone else, with high pitched voices of excitement.

The members of the family took their seats, and a hearty supper and lively conversation were enjoyed by all. The children finished their food directly and, like all children, were begging to be excused from the table so they could go play. James and Roslynd encouraged them to stay in their seats until everyone else was finished, but their encouragement only lasted a moment before they were forced to offer another round. The couple's attention was constantly turned to their children, though they were still able to actively engaged with the rest of the party.

Elizabeth watched the children with pleasure, enjoying the sound of every laugh and giggle. She understood their excitement at being in a new place. If the party was smaller, and her every move not under the scrutiny of everyone, she would join them in their excitement. As it was, she was just considering her good fortune and hoping the tides of the party's malice were parting when she heard the unpleasant sound of her mother's nervous complaining.

"How can you allow your children to be so unruly? Do you take delight in vexing me? You have no compassion on my poor nerves," Mrs. Bennet squawked at Lady Roslynd as her daughter let loose a shrill giggle in response to her brother's teasing. All eyes turned in Mrs. Bennet's direction, though no one responded, unsure of what to say. Mrs. Bennet took it as an invitation to continue. "You do not know what I suffer. Why, these little children running helter-skelter all around the manor, screaming and causing a ruckus, has done nothing but disturb my equanimity. Here, I thought we would have an enjoyable holiday in the quiet and solitude of the north, and what do we get? The most ill-behave and unruly children I have ever laid eyes on. Why, even Elizabeth acted better than they do, and I daresay she was a horrid child. Almost the death of—"

Everyone had been sitting in shock, but her final decree regarding Elizabeth put Fitzwilliam to action. "Madame, you have said quite enough."

Lady Roslynd stood with tears in her eyes and fled from the room before anyone could stop her. Her husband stood to follow, but Elizabeth waved him down. Looking straight at her mother, she said, "Thank you for your visit, Mother; it was nice to see you again. I will be sorry to see you go. However, I understand the company we have chosen to enjoy our Christmas with is not to your liking. I hope your journey home is a safe one." Then, turning to Lady Matlock, she asked, "Aunt Lillian, I would appreciate it if you would accompany me upstairs to attend Roslynd."

Lady Matlock said not a word but stood and followed Elizabeth from the room.

It took some effort, but finally Elizabeth and Lady Matlock were able to coax Roslynd from her room and convince her to come downstairs. When she entered the drawing room, she walked straight into the arms of her worried husband. He had wanted to go to her a multitude of times during the course of the past hour, but the gentlemen had urged him to stay and let the ladies work it out.

Elizabeth glanced around the room for her mother and father but did not see them. As she reached Fitzwilliam's, side he leaned over and whispered in her ear, "Your parents are in their room. Your father wishes to speak with you as soon as you are able. He has informed the stables that he *may* call for the carriage to take them to Lambton, but I believe he hopes a compromise can be reached. Shall we go to them?"

Elizabeth nodded.

Fitzwilliam excused the two of them for a few minutes, stating they had matters to attend to, but the whole party knew exactly where they were going.

Elizabeth took a deep breath and steadied her hands before knocking. It was still on the other side of the door, but no sooner had the echo of her knock ceased than it swung wide. Her father stood on the other side. *He must have been standing at the door waiting*, thought Elizabeth.

The distress on Mr. Bennet's face was

obvious to Elizabeth's trained eyes. She was her father's favourite, as everyone knew, and being sent away from her new home on account of his thoughtless wife angered him more than he was willing to admit.

His wife's foolishness had long irritated him, but he chose to ignore her rather than take her to task for her silliness. Never did he dream her actions would cause him so much pain. For the first time, he felt regret over how he had handled her these past twenty years complete.

"Elizabeth, Mr. Darcy," Mr. Bennet nodded his head to the two standing just outside his room, "would you like to come in?"

"Yes, Father." Elizabeth and Fitzwilliam stepped into the Bennets' bed chamber. Mrs. Bennet sat rigid in a chair near the fire, her hands clasped in her lap, a hard expression on her face.

"Lizzy, I am certain everyone misunderstood what I was saying."

Elizabeth raised her hand to silence her mother. "Mother, no one misunderstood. Everyone perfectly comprehended the meaning of your slight against the Fitzwilliam children. I know it is difficult for you to refrain from upsetting those around you." Elizabeth frowned at her mother's reaction. "Do not look at me that way. This is not Longbourn. These people are not acquainted with your ways. You may say and do anything you like in your own home, but here at Pemberley you will refrain from criticizing my servants and guests or you will leave. Have I made myself clear?"

Elizabeth glared at her mother, daring her to question her authority. Mr. Bennet and Fitzwilliam each stood in silence, watching the conversation with rapt attention. Mr. Bennet had known the day would come when Elizabeth would give her mother a sitting-down. He had seen the tension building between the two for years, but never had he anticipated it would happen after such an event. Mrs. Bennet slighting a family of such distinction could damage the Bennet family standing in London and throughout the country. Though Mr. Bennet did not enjoy spending time in town, he needed to sell his produce, and every businessman knows one must maintain a solid reputation to get the best prices in London.

Mr. Bennet's ears perked at the sound of his wife's hoarse reply. "Perfectly."

Elizabeth locked eyes with her mother and nodded at her response. Neither said a word; Elizabeth did not want to scold her mother more than necessary, and Mrs. Bennet feared saying the wrong thing.

Finally, Mr. Bennet's tentative voice was heard. "Elizabeth, is it asking too much to give your mother one final opportunity to behave herself?"

Elizabeth slowly turned her eyes from her mother to her father. "I do not know, Father. I would love to give Mother another chance, but it has been no more than twenty-four hours since she slighted a servant, not to mention all the times she has demeaned me, which I have been willing to overlook."

Mr. Bennet bowed his head with sadness. To his chagrin, Elizabeth was correct and had every right to ask them to leave her home. He feared if they left under such circumstances they would never be allowed to visit again, and nothing distressed him more than the thought of losing the right to visit his dearest girl. "You are, of course, correct. We will gather our things and depart immediately."

Elizabeth let out an exasperated breath. "Father, I do not want you to leave. I prefer that Mother would take the trouble to understand the pain she causes to others and keep her malicious thoughts in her silly head." Turning to her mother, she spoke directly to her. "If you think you can behave yourself for the rest of your visit, I would be happy to let you stay, but, so help me God, if you misbehave one more time you will be asked to leave and I will not regret it."

"Oh yes, Lizzy, I promise I will behave. Thank you for giving me this opportunity to prove myself. I will not let you down." Mrs. Bennet had been relieved when Elizabeth had changed her mind and allowed them to stay. She feared her husband's response if they were sent away.

"Well, my dear," said Mr. Bennet, "if your daughter should have reason to be distressed and if she should ask us to leave, it would be a comfort to know it was all because you allowed your nerves to run away with you."

"Oh! I am not afraid of upsetting her. I have learned my lesson and will be on my best behaviour for the rest of our stay. I dare say she will be glad we have come to spend Christmas together."

Elizabeth, feeling really very anxious, was determined to leave her parents in their room. Though Mrs. Bennet had offered her assurances, Elizabeth in no way believed her mother would be able to hold her tongue. "Fitzwilliam and I must attend our guests. We would be happy if you would join us when you think you have a proper apology prepared for Lady Fitzwilliam. A simple, to the point apology is best; be sincere, but please do not overdo it or make another scene."

Mr. Bennet understood his daughter's meaning and assured her he would help her mother prepare to enter company. He kissed her cheek and sincerely thanked her for allowing them to remain before closing the door behind her and her husband.

As the door closed, Elizabeth melted into Fitzwilliam's arms. He offered her the support she needed as he wrapped his sturdy arms around her. "There, there, Elizabeth. You did what you must. Your father understands and will not fault you for having to take your mother to task. In fact, I think a part of him regrets that you must."

"I know, but it is still hard. I wish she did not act as she does. At times, I fear she is sillier and more ignorant than Kitty and Lydia."

Fitzwilliam chuckled. "Perhaps we should

give her credit. It is surely a marvelous feat to be that silly."

Elizabeth rolled her eyes as they walked down the hall. "Your jokes are not funny, Fitzwilliam. A mother should never be sillier than her adolescent daughters."

## Chapter 9

Just when Elizabeth was sure there could be no more surprises, she heard her sister exclaim while looking out the window, "La, Lizzy, who is coming up the drive?"

"I do not know; we are not expecting anyone else. For heaven's sake, we were not expecting more than half of you." Walking to the window, Elizabeth looked out to see an impressive carriage coming up the drive. As it entered the gate, a foreboding sense of doom swept over Elizabeth. Emblazoned on the side of the carriage was the de Bourgh family crest.

Had Elizabeth been alone, she would have groaned aloud, but as it was, all she could do was smile. "It seems we may have the pleasure of having Lady Catherine de Bourgh and her daughter, Miss Anne de Bourgh, as well."

Lady Matlock rushed to the window. "I cannot believe it. Catherine rarely leaves Rosings Park, and never in the winter. She would not dream of bringing Anne out in this weather."

The whole party rushed to the foyer as the carriage pulled up at the bottom of the stairs. The butler opened the door to reveal Miss Anne de Bourgh. The party looked behind her in anticipation of the arrival of Lady Catherine, but she did not appear.

Anne greeted everyone warmly and noticed their surreptitious glances into the carriage interior. "You will not find Mamma with me, for I have come alone."

"Alone!" exclaimed Lady Matlock. "How in the world did you manage that?"

Anne looked at her aunt, slightly irritated that everyone thought her utterly helpless at eight and twenty. In a bold and uncharacteristic way, she stated, "Simple. I kissed Mamma's cheek, called for the carriage, and told the driver Pemberley was my destination. Three days later, *voilà*, here I am."

Most of the party stood in shock, watching Anne. Elizabeth found her voice first. "Come, we must get you in where it is warm. We shall all catch our deaths standing so close to the door in the cold."

Mrs. Reynolds helped Miss de Bourgh remove her outerwear. Elizabeth then led her towards the guest chambers, accompanied by Lady Matlock and Georgiana. Pausing a moment, she leaned towards Mrs. Reynolds and whispered, "Please tell Mr. Darcy his cousin Miss Anne de Bourgh has arrived. If you will, please stress she arrived alone. Also, please send up a tray with some tea and light refreshments, and a maid to assist her."

"Very well, Madame."

"I do hope your journey was pleasant, Anne," Lady Matlock said.

"Yes, it was quite comfortable. We made several stops to rest at inns along the way, and the footman saw that I had plenty of warm blankets and warming stones."

"I am glad the footman looked after you, though I cannot help but wonder that your mother allowed you to come so far alone, and in such weather. Why did Mrs. Jenkinson not accompany you?"

"Mrs. Jenkinson is visiting her family for Christmas. I received Georgiana's invitation but four days ago." Anne looked towards a startled Georgiana, silently begging her to go along with the ruse. Luckily for Anne, Georgiana was quick to agree when the entire party looked to her for confirmation.

"Yes, well, the invitation was sent before I knew how many people would be here at Pemberley. I wanted Anne to come, but I never dreamed Aunt Catherine would allow her. That is why I never mentioned it."

Anne became visibly relieved at Georgiana's response. She would be sure to thank her when next they were alone.

Elizabeth looked at Georgiana skeptically but said not a word. She may not know her new sister well, but she had a gift for discerning when her younger sisters were fibbing, and Georgiana exuded all of the same signs.

"I for one am extremely glad you have come. It is about time your mother let you out in the world," Lady Matlock said.

"Thank you, Aunt. I am very glad I am here, too."

When they arrived at Anne's hastily-prepared room, Elizabeth opened the door and allowed Miss de Bourgh and Lady Matlock to enter ahead of her. Georgiana followed Elizabeth into the room. "Miss de Bourgh—" Elizabeth began.

"Please, call me Anne," Anne interrupted.

"Anne, some tea and refreshments will be up shortly. In addition, I have called for a maid to help you change if you desire. Take your time, and then join us in the drawing room, I am sure Fitzwilliam and the rest of the family will want to see you."

Anne smiled; that was exactly what she was counting on. She dearly hoped one man in particular would be happy to see her, for she was certainly excited at the possibility of seeing Colonel Richard Fitzwilliam.

All of the ladies turned to leave the room, but Anne called out to Georgiana, "Georgie, will you stay with me? I would love to speak with you."

Georgiana nodded and stayed behind while the others left the room.

"Fitzwilliam," Elizabeth called as she entered the library where all the men were gathered, "may I speak with you?"

"Certainly, my love. If you gentlemen will excuse me," he said as he stood and followed

Elizabeth from the room towards his private study.

As soon as the door closed behind them, Elizabeth let out a ragged breath. "You cannot even begin to imagine the dread I felt when I realized it was a Rosings Park carriage that had pulled up in the drive. I actually thought Lady Catherine had come to spoil our Christmas."

"Mrs. Reynolds informed me when Anne arrived. You should have seen the look of shock upon the faces of the gentlemen when I told them. Only your father kept a straight face, and I am sure it is only because he does not know the lady himself. Do you seriously believe she allowed Anne to come alone? I am suspicious."

"I am as well. She assures all of us that Georgiana invited her and that her mother let her come, but to be honest I do not believe it, even after Georgiana confirmed her story."

"Did you say Georgiana invited her?" Fitzwilliam was shocked his sister would extend an invitation without first asking him, especially so soon after his wedding.

"Yes, that is what they claim."

"I agree, something is not right. All we

can do is trust them for now, but be ready for Lady Catherine to arrive at any time."

Elizabeth tensed at the thought of Lady Catherine arriving at Pemberley. She certainly hoped the lady would not come, but she would be ready for her if she did.

Fitzwilliam opened his arms, and Elizabeth stepped into them, leaning her head against his chest as he wrapped his arms around her in an engulfing hug.

"I know this Christmas is not turning out how you originally planned, but I think the liveliness around Pemberley is incredible. This estate has been too quiet for far too long."

Elizabeth looked up lovingly into his eyes as he bowed his head low to kiss her soft lips.

"Fitzwilliam, I know you are right. I just cannot shake the feeling that something catastrophic is going to happen. Will my mother offend your aunt? Will my sisters destroy more artifacts? Will my father disagree with Lord Matlock? Will I live up to Lillian's and Roslynd's expectations of how the Mistress of Pemberley should keep house? Now, on top of it all, I have to worry about the possible arrival of Lady Catherine.

Oh, can you imagine her and my mother together for an entire week? Lord help me!"

Fitzwilliam chuckled and tightened his arms around Elizabeth, "You have nothing to worry about. Who cares if your mother and my aunt do not get along? Who cares if your father and my uncle disagree? Georgiana is entertaining your sisters, and now that Anne is here my aunt and Roslynd have someone to fuss over. I dare say, your mother will follow suit. In addition," here he took Elizabeth's face in his hands and looked deep into her eyes, making sure he had her full attention, "the only person who has any say about how the Mistress of Pemberley should keep house is the Mistress of Pemberley herself."

Elizabeth heaved a sigh and said, "I know you are right, but I cannot help worrying. I want your family to accept me."

"You have nothing to fear. Remember, my aunt and uncle only care that we made a love match. They are here more out of curiosity than to approve or disapprove. Regardless, I care not what they think."

"I do!" Elizabeth exclaimed. Fitzwilliam gave her a scolding look. He began to address her, but she stopped him. "There is no point arguing over it, for we will never agree. Come, we must gather everyone in the drawing room. I think Anne will not take long to come down to see everyone."

"Are you sure she is not too tired? I think she may need her rest."

Elizabeth looked at him with a shrewd expression. "I highly doubt your cousin is as sickly as her mother makes her out to be. She looked remarkably well upon her arrival here, and not tired at all."

Fitzwilliam followed Elizabeth from the study towards the drawing room were all of the gentlemen had already gathered with the ladies.

"Oh, Georgie, thank heavens you did not out me. I am so relieved."

"Anne, why in the world are you here, and where is your mother? She would not have let you come alone. You must tell me at once."

Just then there was a knock on the door. Anne held her finger to her lips, silencing Georgiana. "Enter," she called.

A rosy-cheeked maid came in with a laden tray and bobbed a curtsey. "Good day, miss. Mrs. Darcy asked me to bring up this tea tray for you. Would you like me to leave it on this little table?"

"Yes, that is a fine place to set it."

The maid carefully set the tray down and addressed Miss de Bourgh again. "Mrs. Darcy also wants to ensure you have all the assistance you need in preparations for coming below stairs. Would you like me to help you with your hair or gown?"

"No, I will be fine; my cousin will assist me."

Georgiana nodded in agreement. The maid curtsied again and left the room, closing the door behind her.

"I hope it is all right, Georgie. I thought it would give us more time to talk."

"Yes, but you must promise to tell me all."

"Let's see, where to begin?" Anne paused a moment to collect her thoughts. "I guess it all started last September when your brother chose to marry Elizabeth instead of me."

"But I thought you did not love Fitzwilliam?"

"You are correct, I do not love him as anything more than a cousin, but do not forget that my mother has had her heart set on my marrying him since the day I was born."

Georgiana nodded in understanding.

Anne continued. "Almost from the first moment she received Fitzwilliam's letter announcing his engagement, she has been determined to marry me off to the first rich suitor she can find. Oh, Georgie, you should see the dastardly men she has been inviting to Rosings Park. I am tired of it. I know my own mind, and I know who I want to marry. I have come to Pemberley because he is here."

"What? Here!" Georgiana exclaimed. "Who is he?"

Anne giggled a little. "Think about it. Who here is single and of marrying age?"

Georgiana paused a moment in thought until her eyes lit up and the words rushed from her mouth. "Richard! You are in love with Richard!"

"I most certainly am. When I think back on it, I am sure I have loved him for the past ten years at least."

"Ten years! But why have you never said anything before?"

"Because your brother has never been married before. Mother would never agree to such a marriage if Fitzwilliam was still available. I highly doubt she will agree to it now, but I have a better chance than before."

"I think it is a lovely idea. Do you know if he returns your affection?"

Anne's face fell. "I do not know. I am sure he enjoys my company, for every year at Easter we spend much time together; however, I am unsure if that is because I'm the only person around or he truly wants to be with me. I have come here to take control of my destiny and to find out once and for all if he loves me, and if we can be happy together."

The two cousins partook of the light refreshments and then quickly readied Anne to appear downstairs for her visit with the entire family.

When the ladies entered the drawing room, all eyes turned to them. The gentlemen stood, and Richard rushed to their sides to be the first to address Anne. "Anne, what a pleasure it is to have you here. Why, nothing could have prepared me for the shock I received upon Fitzwilliam telling us you had arrived. I assure you, nothing could make me happier than knowing you will be spending Christmas with us. Is it true your mother actually let you come alone?"

Anne laughed at his shock. Nothing could please her more than to receive such attention from him. "Why is it no one believes me when I say that mother let me come alone?" Georgiana knowingly smiled as Richard offered Anne his arm. The two had only taken a few steps when Lord Matlock's commanding voice was heard.

"Because we all know your mother," he replied as he stood and gave his niece a hug. "I agree with everyone, though; it is indeed a pleasure to have you here with us."

Richard led Anne to the chair by the fire. Once she was situated, he pulled a second chair close to her and sat down.

The rest of the afternoon was spent by the family getting to know one another better.

Mary and Kitty joined Georgiana sitting near the window. Georgiana secretly told them to keep an eye on the blossoming romance between her cousins Anne and Richard. Nothing could satisfy the trio more than a budding romance, and for the remainder of the afternoon they watched the pair for any and all signs of admiration. Each time Anne leaned close to speak to him, and whenever Richard laughed at something she said, the girls winked at each other and smiled. Georgiana was happy for her cousin, for if her observations of the two were anything to make a judgment on, she was sure Richard returned Anne's affections.

# Chapter 10

Elizabeth slept ill and woke Sunday with pains in her hips and neck. Sitting up in bed, she rolled her head from side to side trying to work out the stiffness. She winced at the pain, but continued the motions, understanding that all she needed was to get up and use her joints and muscles.

"Are you well, my dear?" Fitzwilliam asked when he saw Elizabeth stretching in an uncharacteristic manner.

"Yes, I am well, just a little sore. I'm afraid I did not sleep at all last night. All of the tossing and turning must have done me more harm than good."

Fitzwilliam sat up and kneaded her shoulder and back muscles with his strong hands. Elizabeth sighed against him, his gentle ministrations working wonders on her aching body.

"You had best be careful; I am likely to make a habit out of this." Elizabeth teased. "I did not realize my shoulders hurt so badly until you began massaging them. I hurt everywhere!"

Fitzwilliam increased the intensity of his massaging, working his hands over her shoulders, neck, and back. The combined efforts of his ministrations and her gentle sighs wreaked havoc on his masculine composure.

When Elizabeth gave one final sigh and leaned back into his embrace, he accepted her and wrapped his arms tightly around her. Pulling her close, he kissed her temple and breathed in her womanly scent. He loved the smell of her. His body craved her as he had every minute since they had married.

"Fitzwilliam, do we honestly have to get up? I would prefer to linger here in bed with you."

"This is your house; you may do anything you choose. If you want to stay in bed all day, I will join you." He lay back down, pulling Elizabeth with him, and then swept the covers back over them. Elizabeth giggled in his arms.

"Nothing would please me more, my dear,

but I suspect we cannot. Can you imagine what my mother would say if she knew we had stayed in bed all day, together?"

Fitzwilliam laughed. "I do not care what your mother would say. This is my house, I will do as I choose."

Elizabeth thought for a moment. "I'm trying to decide if I care or not. Normally I do not care what my mother thinks; however, I dread hearing her opinion voiced to the entire household. No, I think we must get up. She was polite and did not cause a scene yesterday, but I doubt her good behaviour would last under such temptation."

She turned to face Fitzwilliam, wrapped her arms around him, and pressed her lips to his. Then she rose and stepped from the bed, calling Gracie to assist in her preparations for the day. Today was Sunday, and Elizabeth planned on wearing one of her new gowns. This would be the Darcys' first Sunday in attendance at the Pemberley Chapel since their marriage, and she was sure to meet many of the Pemberley tenants and families from the surrounding area. Elizabeth wanted to make a favourable impression on all of them.

The Sunday services were beautiful. With the Christmas season upon them, the parson had delivered a heartfelt sermon about keeping hope alive. Elizabeth had been touched by the sermon, and as the final notes of the closing hymn rang through the walls of the chapel, she linked her arm through Fitzwilliam's and rested her head upon his shoulder.

She had so many hopes for the coming year.

At the conclusion of the services, the whole party returned to Pemberley and spent the afternoon in their different pursuits of enjoyment. Elizabeth and Mrs. Reynolds had laid out holiday crafts for the Fitzwilliam children, and provided ample lace, ribbons, and adornments for Georgiana, Mary, and Kitty to trim their gowns and bonnets. Needlework and yarn was provided to the ladies, and the Pemberley library was opened to the gentlemen.

Hardly anyone noticed the couple who were missing.

Anne had been at Pemberley less than twenty-four hours when she contrived a method to get Richard alone. "Richard, the sun is glorious today. I would love to take a walk in the Orangery. I have heard of its beauty and delights and would like to experience it. Would you accompany me?"

"It would be my pleasure," said Richard as he stood from his chair and offered Anne his arm. The two left the room together.

Their walk towards the Orangery began in silence, as Anne was somewhat distracted. Richard observed the constant activity of her free hand.

"Anne, what is the matter?"

Anne looked towards Richard with eyes full of interest. "Nothing. Why would you ask such a question?"

"No reason," Richard said. He continued to observe her from the corner of his eye, not believing her.

"I am glad Mother allowed me to come to Pemberley for Christmas." Anne rushed her speech, eager to occupy the silence and Richard's inquisitive mind with other matters.

"As we all are. The entire family is pleased to have you here with us."

Anne was little pleased with his response. "Are *you* happy I am here?"

"Of course I am. Why would I not be?"

Anne rolled her eyes at her dense cousin.

He had not understood her meaning at all. "I know you are happy that so many of your family are together for Christmas, but, Richard, answer me this. Are you happier that I am here because I represent another member of your family, or because it is me?"

Richard paused in the hallway and looked down at Anne. He had long thought Lady Catherine had fixed her sights on the wrong cousin. For many years now he had wished he was in Fitzwilliam's position, the eldest son in line to inherit Pemberley. He did not want Fitzwilliam's place for wealth and influence; he wanted it for the prospective bride. Almost from her birth, Lady Catherine had fixed Fitzwilliam as Anne's intended, and, though neither of them wanted the match, nothing else had been talked of for close to twenty-eight years.

For the past eight years, at least, Richard had thought of little else than becoming the husband of Anne, though, until this fall, he had feared it could never happen. As long as Fitzwilliam remained single, Lady Catherine would continue to believe his marriage to Anne would still take place.

Once Fitzwilliam had announced his intention to marry Elizabeth, Richard's hope soared until a few days later when he had gone to Matlock to visit his parents and overheard them discussing a letter from Lady Catherine. They were agreeing it would be best if Lady Catherine brought Anne to London and gave her a proper coming out. They thought Anne deserved the chance for a little scene and society. If Anne came to London, as a rich heiress of an age considered well past marriageability she would be preyed upon by all manner of fortune hunters. There were many men who would take advantage of her situation, and before she or Lady Catherine would even consider the possibility of a ruse, Anne would be married off to the rogue.

In his mind, he had recited a hundred marriage proposals to Anne over the years, but none of them had been accepted. For the first time, he truly hoped.

Richard chose his words carefully as he responded to Anne. "Anne," he said, looking straight into her eyes, "nothing pleases me more, as a single man, then to have a beautiful single woman here, and for that woman to be *you*."

Anne blushed under his attention; it was just as she had hoped. They resumed their walk to the Orangery in silence, Anne's grasp of his arm a little tighter.

Richard opened the door and allowed her to enter ahead of him. He heard her gasp as she took in the sight before her. "Oh, Richard, this place is lovely. I have heard of the beauty of this building, but never had I imagined it so exquisite as this." Anne looked up at the glass ceiling that allowed the light of the sun to shine through uninhibited. Rushing in, she twirled around and breathed deep the perfume of the flowers all around her. She rushed from one flower to the next, bending to take in the scent of each.

Richard watched her flutter around the plants, amusement playing across his face. He was already beginning to think of her as *his* Anne, and calculating how he could spend his life making her smile. Seeing her pleasure in the place brought him sheer joy. Finally, she calmed down a little and returned to his side.

"So, you like the place, do you?"

"Yes!" was her emphatic reply. "I think someday I will commission a building just like this at Rosings Park." Her statement brought him slightly back to reality. If she believed she would be at Rosings Park forever, certainly she had never considered a life as the wife of a military man a possibility.

"I am sure it will be lovely," Richard said.

Anne looked towards him, a little unsure of his less than enthusiastic reply. "Do you not think it is a good idea?"

"Yes, I think it is a splendid idea." Richard could see the apprehension in her face and tried to raise his enthusiasm, if for nothing more than to see her smile return.

It worked; a smile returned to Anne's face. Reaching for his hand, Anne practically dragged Richard to the back of the Orangery. Sitting on a large rock near the fountain, she let her fingers play in the cold water. Richard stood near her, watching her.

"You know," she said, "I have frequently heard about this building from Georgiana and your mother, but I could never express any interest in it. If I had, my mother would assume I looked forward to seeing the room as Fitzwilliam's bride." Anne looked at Richard, who stood stoic, listening to her. She then returned her attention to her fingers playing in the water as she continued. "I have lived in misery for twenty-eight years, everyone assuming I would marry him. You know, neither he nor I have ever wanted to marry one another. We talked about it when we were both young, and then again when we were eighteen. Although we respect each other, we have never had any inclination to love one another as a husband and wife ought." Anne looked at him again, trying to summon the courage to tell him what she had come to Pemberley to say.

Richard's mind was racing with dates. She had been eighteen ten years ago. She had known for ten years that she would not marry Fitzwilliam. Fitzwilliam had known the entire time. It was only four years ago that Fitzwilliam had informed him he would not marry Anne. Until then, even he had thought Fitzwilliam was considering it. Richard thought about the past eight years since he had realized he loved Anne. He enjoyed being in society, attending balls and parties, and receiving the attention of the ladies, but it had always seemed a little hollow, a little fake to him. He was ashamed of himself for trifling with ladies' affections when his heart was already engaged. He was frustrated he could not go to the lady he loved and just tell her so. Could he do it now? He wanted to, and it seemed she wanted it too. Would their family object? Did either of them care?

"Anne," Richard's voice was barely a whisper, "why have you never told me this before? For ten years you have known you would not marry Fitzwilliam. For ten years we have shared Easter together, rides in your phaeton, and walks around Rosings Park, but still you did not mention that you never intended to marry him."

His quiet voice sounded accusatory, and Anne feared she had hurt him. Her tone rose as she answered him. "Do not put the blame on me. You do not know what it is like to live with my mother, constantly in fear of what she will say or do. Even now that Fitzwilliam has been married almost a month, I fear of telling her what it is I want. Do you know why I am here? Do you want to know the truth?" Anne was upset, her voice raised almost to the point of yelling. All Richard could do was nod in response. He had known she was hiding something, and it seemed he was about to find out what. "I ran away."

His surprise was complete. He did not know what he had expected her to say, but this was not it.

"Yes, that is right, I ran away. After mother had gone to bed, I ordered carriage and left under the cloak of darkness. I was past London before I called for the coach to break, fearing Mother would discover me gone and head straight there. The following day I made it to Leicester, and then here."

"Anne, what have you done?" Richard questioned, fear in his voice.

"Done? Richard, of all people I hoped you would understand me. Support me."

"I do. It is just that I fear your mother will arrive here at any time."

"No, she has no idea where I have gone, and she will never come this far north in the winter."

"Come, we must speak to my father." Richard stood to leave, beckoning Anne to follow him, but she would not. She stayed sitting on her rock.

"No, I have not finished. I have come to Pemberley for a purpose, and I intend to fulfill it. If I do not do it now, I fear I will lose my courage."

Richard stopped and turned back to her. "Purpose?"

Anne let out the breath she held. "Richard, my true goal was to see *you*, and to judge whether I might ever hope to make you love me. For the past ten years I have loved no one but you. You are the only man I could love as a woman should love her husband. I have come here to tell you, and to find out if you could love me in return." Anne stood and rushed past Richard towards the door. He reached for her as she passed him, but he missed. She was almost at the door before he caught up with her.

"Anne," he called as he caught her arm and halted her progress. "You love me?"

She nodded and lowered her eyes to her fidgeting hands in front of her. Richard drew her into his arms and, without warning, pressing his lips against hers.

Anne's arms wrapped around him as she drank in his hot kisses and matched his ardor.

As his lips released hers, he asked, "Why did you never tell me?"

"Fear."

"What do you have to fear from me? I would never hurt you."

"You would hurt my heart if you did not love me in return."

They shared another kiss and then sought out a bench to sit on. The next two hours were spent enjoying their newfound mutual love and considering possibilities for the future.

## Chapter 11

Georgiana, Mary, and Kitty had been almost inseparable since Friday when they had once again found themselves together after a few short weeks of separation. Georgiana had longed for sisters most of her life, and now that Fitzwilliam had married Elizabeth, she was in the happy position of gaining not only one, but several.

She enjoyed her cousin Anne's company immensely; however, the gap of twelve years in their ages was a barrier that was not often breached. Anne may have broken down and shared that she was in love with their cousin Richard, but since then the two had barely spoken except in the company of the whole family.

Georgiana had shared Anne's secret with Mary and Kitty, and the three had spent the past day and a half observing every move the couple made in company. This morning it was apparent to all three that the couple had declared themselves and had found their feelings mutual. They had not yet shared their happy news with the family, but anyone willing to open their eyes and see beyond their own situation would see a couple in love.

The three often found themselves in deep conversation about when they would find true love and what they expected from it. They knew for a fact they would not marry without love, for who would ever settle for anything except true love after seeing the happiness Jane and Elizabeth had found with Charles and Fitzwilliam, and now Anne and Richard.

At first Kitty was determined to marry a military man like Lydia had, and Mary thought no one but a clergyman would suit her, but soon Georgiana had changed their minds with tales of the friends her brother had brought to Pemberley over the years. In due time, all of the girls had decided that gentleman, tradesmen, military, or clergy mattered not, so long as the man was handsome and loved them with his entire heart, might, mind, and soul.

Anne and Richard once again escaped the company of the family in favour of a walk together through the halls of Pemberley.

It did not take long for Anne's spirits to rise to playfulness, and she wanted Richard to account for his having ever fallen in love with her. "How could you begin?" said she. "I can comprehend your going on charmingly, when you had once made a beginning; but what could set you off in the first place?"

"I cannot fix on the hour, or the spot, or the look, or the words, which laid the foundation. It is too long ago. I was in the middle before I knew I *had* begun."

"Oh, how horrid that you should have such a response. I would rather learn of a single moment when my beauty became irresistible. That you no longer thought of me as your cousin, but rather from that day forward nothing but your wife would do. I would like to hear how you have pined away for years, wondering if I loved you as you love me. Come, Richard, you must give me something. A woman wants to know how long she has been loved."

"Oh, Anne, how pretentious you are today. What if I told you I was in love with you for most of the years I visited Rosings Park with Fitzwilliam at Easter?" Anne's mind raced to count how many years Richard had come to Rosings, but her calculations were interrupted as he continued. "Why, I have loved you since before I realized your sickness was no more than an act to keep your mother at bay."

"Now, do not you go telling anyone that. I plan on using that ace to manipulate my mother for years to come."

"What I do not understand is how you can take all of the medicine she insists you take and not get sick from it."

Leaning towards him, as if to convey a deep secret, Anne loudly whispered, "Ah, now there is a trick for you. My doctor has known of my ruse for years. There is nothing but a variety of coloured juices or water in my medicine bottles, and the tablets are no more than sweets from London."

"You are a sly thing, are you not? How did you ever get him to go along with such a scheme?"

"That was easy. He hates it when mother advises him how to do his job. The more she advises, the more willing he is to deceive her.

I believe it brings him utter joy to know we have tricked her for so many years."

"What about your companion? Does she know?"

"Mrs. Jenkinson? Heavens no, and you had better not tell her. She is loyal to no one but my mother. Certainly I do not need such a companion at eight and twenty, but mother swears she has been with us so long that she will not be dismissed until I am married."

"What about you? Can you fix a time or place to when you fell in love with me?"

"I wondered if you were going to ask me, so last night I thought back, and yes, I believe I know exactly when I realized I loved you as a man and not as a cousin."

Richard's eyebrows rose as he asked her, "When?"

"It was about ten years ago. I had just turned eighteen. You had come with Fitzwilliam for Easter and we were playing croquet on the south lawn near the pond. You were attempting to demonstrate the mightiness of your swing when your ball went errant into the pond, and then you went in after it."

"Heaven forbid, did you peek?"

Anne laughed out loud at his crimson

face. "Of course I did. Every self-respecting woman would have."

"I specifically remember I told you to turn around and cover your face while I retrieved the ball."

"Oh, I did exactly as you requested until you turned your back to me. It was then that I peeked, multiple times." Richard groaned in embarrassment as she continued. "I had never seen a man's bare back before, and though I enjoyed the view, it was the sight of your wet torso coming out of the water that excited me most. You know, I have experienced a repeat of the event in my dreams at least fifty times. Each dream is more realistic and better than the one before it. Last night I had the dream again, but it was different. Do you want to know why it was different?"

Richard knew the question was baited, but he could not resist answering in the affirmative.

"Generally my dream ends when you step from the pond onto land and put your shirt and cravat back on. Not last night, though. You walked up to me," Anne walked towards Richard, "just like this. Then I placed my hands right here," Anne placed her hands flat against his chest, "and you wrapped your arms around me," here she smiled as he wrapped his arms around her, "and we kissed."

"Like this?" Richard questioned, leaning over to share a passionate kiss with her.

"Mmm, yes, just like that."

"Did you enjoy your dream?"

"Of course. I always enjoy my dreams when you are in them."

"I am in them often, then?" said he.

"Not as often as I wish. You always occupy them when you are most on my mind. The weeks preceding, during, and after your Easter visits always featured you in them, but the longer you are absent or the less I hear about you, the further you are from them. The last two nights you have been their focus, and, lucky for me, the dreams have been heated and intense."

"If you were eighteen when you realized you loved me, was it the same Easter you and Fitzwilliam decided you would never marry?"

Anne nodded.

"The answer does not matter, but did you love me before or after the two of you agreed never to marry?"

"If it does not matter, perhaps I should not answer your question," Anne teased. She could see by the look on his face he dearly wanted to know. Whether he realized it or not, the answer to the question was paramount. Had she begun to love him because Fitzwilliam had broken her heart, or had she loved him already and was relieved that Fitzwilliam did not want to marry her?

"It is entirely up to you, my dear, but I am curious about your answer."

"Well, then, I shall humour you and let you in on my little secret." She drew close to him, looked straight into his eyes, and said, "I was already in love with you. In fact, it was I who prompted the conversation with Fitzwilliam." Relief spread through Richard. He knew it was foolish, but part of him wanted her love all to himself. She may love only him now, but to know she had loved Fitzwilliam in the past, even for a short time, was unthinkable. Anne did not know it, but she had settled all of his fears when she offered one final affirmation. "I could never have loved Fitzwilliam. Mother had set her sights on him from the moment of my birth. By the time I knew what love was,

I already detested the possibility of a match with him."

Their common love had unlocked the gates of communication and allowed each insight into certain events from their past that they had previously been uncertain about. Richard could not be satisfied until Anne had repeatedly told him that she could love only him. Lucky for Richard, Anne was happy to manifest her love in more ways than one.

## Chapter 12

By Tuesday morning, the entire party had been in residence almost four days. The disorder was beginning to settle, and Elizabeth imagined Christmas would turn out well after all. Gracie was just putting the finishing touches on her hair when Fitzwilliam entered the room dressed and ready for the day.

"Fitzwilliam," Elizabeth called to draw his attention away from the paper he held in his hands, "have you noticed that Richard and Anne seem to be spending a lot of time alone, away from the family?"

"No, I have not," he said as he set his paper aside and turned his full attention to his wife.

"I noticed they were missing on Sunday, but did not think much of it. Then yesterday when I entered the drawing room where everyone was gathered, they were missing again. The two did not return until it was time to prepare for supper."

"Interesting. I am surprised I did not notice, but then again, perhaps I should not be. I have been extremely busy trying to ensure six grown men have enough amusements to occupy themselves indoors when they would much prefer to be outside. I suppose one missing chap was not noticed by any of us."

"I would like you to pay close attention to him today, and though I am sure all is well, if you feel inclined to investigate I would like to ensure nothing untowards is happening. I trust both Anne and Richard explicitly; however, they are under our roof, and if there is any impropriety we would be to blame."

"Yes, dearest, I agree. I will speak with Richard today."

"Thank you," Elizabeth said as Gracie finished her hair. "I would be distressed if Lady Catherine appeared and had cause to criticize me more than she already does."

"Are you still worried she will come?"

"Of course I am. I will worry until Anne's carriage has arrived safe and sound back at Rosings Park."

"My uncle and I have spoken at length about her being here. If Anne did not come with her mother's permission, Lady Catherine would have arrived long before now."

"I am sure you are right, but I cannot shake the feeling that she will show up at any moment."

"Rest easy. You let me worry about Lady Catherine. Christmas is nearing, and you have more useful things to think about."

"Yes, I suppose I do. Mrs. Lacroix informed me she believes the ham is too small for our party. She has not been able to procure another, and it is too late to have one butchered from Pemberley. I must decide by today if we want to serve both ham and turkey, or if we remove ham altogether and just serve turkey, which we have plenty of."

"Oh, the decisions the mistress must attend to," teased Fitzwilliam. "If I may be of service, I would be happy to provide my opinion on the matter."

"You would?" Elizabeth questioned. "What would your opinion be?"

"I think we should have both."

"Oh, and why do you say that?"

"I think it will provide a more impressive

meal and attest to your skills as mistress of the estate. Additionally, the variety will appeal to the palates of all of our visitors, not to mention the added colour will make the table setting look delightful."

"Since when have you cared about the table setting?"

"Since never, but I have often heard your mother express such things, almost since the first of our acquaintance. Even if your father does not allow her to mention it, I am sure it will not be lost upon her. We must give her some credit, for she does notice every minor detail. I believe she must run a smooth house despite her being prone to nerves."

"I have not given it much thought, but I think you are right. Longbourn is a highly efficient house. I always figured it was because Mrs. Hill was able to keep things under control."

"Lizzy, you cannot have thought that. You know as well as I no matter how adept a servant, the household is run in the manner of the mistress. If Longbourn operates smoothly it is because your mother makes it so."

"No, Fitzwilliam, I guess I did not consider it. I never imagined Longbourn operated as it did because of my mother. I always thought it operated in spite of her."

Fitzwilliam just shook his head as he offered her his arm and escorted her downstairs. The realization of Mrs. Bennet's ability to maintain a household had never dawned on Elizabeth, and now that it had she was searching her memory for insight into how her mother maintained household order. Elizabeth considered that perhaps her mother was correct and she had not paid her half the attention that she should have over the years.

Elizabeth vowed to herself that if the occasion arose, she would take the opportunity to offer her mother praise and perhaps ask a few tips, this time with the purpose of listening to her answers instead of assuming the woman had nothing to teach her.

As Elizabeth entered the breakfast parlour, she was amazed at the assembly before her. Most of the family were already awake and present, including Kitty, who until recently was inclined to sleep as late as her mother would allow. The families were learning to tolerate one another, if not actually enjoying one another's company. Almost two full days had passed without a catastrophe, and Elizabeth was beginning to relax.

Elizabeth had not been the only one expecting Lady Catherine's arrival for the past four days, but still the lady had not arrived. Lady Matlock had just mentioned to her husband that they must be in the clear when Mrs. Reynolds entered the room and bent down next to Mr. and Mrs. Darcy to impart her message.

"Mr. Darcy, sir, I have just been informed another carriage from Rosings Park is coming up the drive. The arrival is imminent."

Looking towards Elizabeth, Fitzwilliam responded, "Thank you, Mrs. Reynolds. We will be right there."

The couple stood without another word, telling looks passing between them. As they reached the hallway, Fitzwilliam offered his arm to his wife and said, "I know we do not want her here, but apparently you were right; she is come. I guess it should not be a surprise that she is here. The surprise is that it took her so long."

"No, it is not a surprise, but no matter how expected she is, it does not change the fact that in five minutes I will wish she had not come."

"Five minutes!" Fitzwilliam chuckled. "You are gracious. I wish her gone already."

Taking a deep, calming breath, Fitzwilliam indicated that the butler should open the door. His timing was impeccable, for a raving Lady Catherine de Bourgh came storming in. "Where is she? Where is my daughter, Anne? I know she must be here."

"Hello, Aunt Catherine. How wonderful it is that you have come to Pemberley to join us for Christmas," said Fitzwilliam.

"I have done no such thing. I planned never to step foot in this house with *her* as mistress." Lady Catherine pointed her walking stick at Elizabeth as she spit the word out. Then she continued her onslaught. "Now, where is my daughter?"

"Aunt, if you will kindly refrain from yelling, and from slighting my *wife*, I would greatly appreciate it." Fitzwilliam's voice was calm and assertive, though it did little to alleviate Lady Catherine's ire.

"I will do no such thing. I have been brought here against my will and my better judgment."

"I assure you, Aunt, no one has brought

you here against your will. Why, you came of your own accord."

"I most certainly did not. I am here only because I have learnt Anne is here. Now, where is she? I must speak to her immediately."

"Ah, I wondered what the ruckus was," exclaimed Lord Matlock as he entered the foyer with Lady Matlock on his arm.

Lady Catherine turned on her brother. "James, what have you done with Anne?"

"Merry Christmas to you, too, sister. I hope you had a pleasant journey?" His manner was stoic and unwavering, which irritated Lady Catherine even more.

"I most certainly did not. You know how I hate to leave Rosings Park, especially in the winter. Nothing but the most urgent business would call me away."

"What did you find so grave as to bring you this far north at this time of year? Of all times to travel, I would have thought you would have avoided December."

"Do not take that insolent tone with me, James. As you well know, Anne is my urgent business."

"Ah, yes, Anne. And how is my sweet niece faring? I hope she is well."

"Do not patronize me. Bring her to me at once!" Lady Catherine was yelling, her voice echoing throughout the manor.

"Lower your voice at once," shouted a clear voice from the top of the stairs. "For heaven's sake, Mother, are you trying to raise the dead?" Anne used a commanding tone none of them had ever heard from her before. Richard was standing at her side, marveling at how each moment she amazed him more and more.

Anne descended the stairs towards her mother with the poise and grace of a sophisticated woman in charge of her own destiny. Her newfound and acknowledged love with Richard had given her the confidence she had lacked for years.

Lady Catherine briskly walked towards her. When they met in the middle of the foyer, Lady Catherine raised her hand and slapped her daughter across the cheek. Richard's reflexes were sharp, and he caught her arm, but not before tears sprang to Anne's eyes. She did not make a sound; instead, she walked past her mother to the front door and addressed the butler. "Please send word to the stables that I would like my carriage ready in an hour."

The entire party stood stunned. No one said a word; they just watched, unable to move. Richard released Lady Catherine's arm, unsure if he should restrain her longer. He stood at the ready to go to Anne's defense again should he need to. Already he felt like taking his aunt to task over her treatment of Anne, but he restrained himself for Anne's sake. She clearly had a plan, and he did not intend to interfere in it.

Turning to Elizabeth, Anne embraced her and said aloud, "Elizabeth, dearest cousin, thank you for hosting me, but I fear I must leave. I do hope you understand and will not refuse me a future invitation on account of my sudden and hasty departure."

Elizabeth returned her embrace and replied, "How could I? You have been such a delightful guest; a room will always be yours, should you ever desire it."

Anne turned to the Matlocks. "Aunt, Uncle, it was a pleasure to see you again. I hope our paths will meet again soon."

Richard's mind was racing. Did she actually intend to leave Pemberley, or was this a bluff? What would he do if she departed? The questions swirled in his mind, then a moment later he answered them without reservation. He would go with her.

Anne then turned to Richard, who stood in the doorway of the drawing room, under the mistletoe. Right there, in front of the assembled party, she arched up on her tiptoes and kissed him full on the mouth. He was shocked at first, but then returned her kiss, resting his hands on her hips.

"Stop that this instant! I will not allow you to ruin your reputation and your prospects with such wanton behavior!" bellowed Lady Catherine.

While the kiss infuriated Lady Catherine, it gave Lady Matlock pause; it was obvious the two had shared a kiss before. Her son looked slightly embarrassed but extremely pleased with himself.

Elizabeth shared an *I told you so* look with Fitzwilliam in regards to their earlier musings about the two.

Lady Matlock stepped into the fray and addressed the entire party. "Let us take a few minutes to get to the bottom of this. Catherine, in the future you will keep your hands to yourself. I had better not catch you striking Anne again, or I will strike you. Am I understood?" Lady Catherine began to object, but Lady Matlock raised her hand to stop her. "Anne, it is too late to begin a journey. I insist you stay at least until tomorrow. I know you do not want to see your mother, and we will all respect your wishes and not force you into company with her, if that is your decision." Anne also began to respond, but Lady Matlock silenced her as well. "Finally, once we get this whole business sorted out," she waved her hand between Lady Catherine and Anne, "we will hear what you two have to say for yourselves." She pointed to Anne and Richard. They would have felt guilty had they not noticed the small smile that graced her lips, but her narrowed eyes meant business and everyone knew not to trifle with her when she had that look about her.

Anne nodded at her aunt immediately, but Lady Catherine stood glaring at her for a full minute. Before she responded to her sister-in-law, she scolded Anne again. "If you leave this manor without my permission, you will be disowned and lose Rosings Park forever. I will not be made a fool running all over the country chasing after an ungrateful daughter."

"Let me be rightly understood, *Mother*."

Anne said the word with disdain. "I am of age and will come and go as I please. You have dictated my life for far too long, and I will not have it anymore."

"Stubborn girl! I am furious with you! Is this how you treat your mother after I have given you everything you ever desired?"

"Everything I ever desired! That is hardly the case, Mother."

"Pray tell me what you have ever desired that I have not provided you," Lady Catherine said with indignation.

"Love, that's what!"

"I love you as much as any mother loves her child."

"That is not the love I am referring to. You have denied me the opportunity to experience the love of a man of my choosing."

"I have already explained that once you join me in London we will find you a suitable husband. He will be a nobleman with wealth and connections. You will come to love him."

"That is not what I want. I want to find true love." Anne spoke with feeling and emotion that few had ever seen in her.

"Anne, I insist that you marry a man who will allow you to continue to live in the manner in which you were raised. I know you would not wish to quit the sphere in which you have been brought up."

"Mother, I have no intention of marrying a man just so I do not have to quit my sphere. I have told you already, I shall marry whom I want, regardless of wealth or connections. Those things do not matter to me. They never have. Now that Fitzwilliam is finally married, I am allowed to express my opinions on the matter without the risk of injuring him."

Fitzwilliam looked sharply at his cousin. "You were not waiting for me, were you?"

"Not in the sense of wanting to marry you. Come, Fitzwilliam, you know better. I was waiting for you to make your choice so Mother would see, once and for all, that you were no longer an option and I should be allowed to make up my own mind."

"Make your own choice?" Lady Catherine spluttered. "How preposterous. Never!"

"Why is that preposterous, Mother? Why should I not make my own choice? It is common for a man and woman to choose one another. Arranged marriages are surely a matter of the past."

"If you intend to live at Rosings Park then you will marry whom I choose for you."

"Perhaps I do not want to live there. I have

been thinking for quite some time now that London may suit me better. I have already inquired with the housekeeper, and though the house in London has not been opened in many years, I only need send a week's notice for it to be prepared."

"Anne, I am shocked and astonished. I expected to find a more reasonable young woman. But do not deceive yourself into a belief that I will ever recede. I shall not go away 'til you have given me the assurance I require."

"And I certainly *never* shall give it. I am not to be intimidated into anything so wholly unreasonable. You may want me to marry some hoity-toity Londoner, but would my giving you the wished-for promise make a marriage at all more probable? Supposing you do find someone willing to marry me, what if I then refused? Would my refusing to accept his hand make him change his mind? I would certainly think so. Allow me to say, Mother, that the arguments with which you have supported this extraordinary application have been as frivolous as the application was ill-judged. You have widely mistaken me if you think I will just marry whomever you chose. I may have been very little out in the world, but I assure you I have been out enough to understand what love is and to know I want it in my marriage. Nay, not want, I demand it in my marriage. I will not marry anyone unless I love him."

"You have no regard, then, for my decisions as your mother! Unfeeling, selfish girl! Do you not consider that a connection with certain persons must disgrace our family in the eyes of everyone?"

"Mother, do you think I care about what *everyone* thinks?"

"You should!"

"No, I should not, and neither should you. You should care for no more than to be happy with the object of my love, and support me in a marriage to him. I am resolved to act in that manner which will, in my own opinion, constitute my happiness without reference to *you* or anyone else."

The banter between Anne and Lady Catherine was intense. Everyone felt they should leave them alone but found they were unable to, so each stood quietly out of the way. Everyone's full attention was on the conversation. Lord Matlock wondered why his sister was so adamant that Anne marry a wealthy Londoner. Why shouldn't she be allowed to marry for love? Elizabeth and Lady Matlock were intently listening for the part that would include Richard, for they both knew he was sure to be mentioned. Richard, however, was dreading the moment he would be noticed, and he was sure that moment was quickly approaching.

"You refuse, then, to oblige me. You refuse to obey the claims of duty, honour, and gratitude. You are determined to ruin yourself, your family name, and the estate, and to make yourself the contempt of the world."

"Neither duty nor honour nor gratitude," replied Anne, "have any possible claim on me in the present instance. No principle of any would be violated by my marriage with a man I love. And with regard to family and friends, I think it is evident in Fitzwilliam's marriage to Elizabeth that the only familial indignation is yours, and no one cares if they lose your good opinion."

"And this is your real opinion! This is your final resolve! Very well. I shall now know how to act. Do not imagine, Anne, that your ambition will ever be gratified. I came to Pemberley with the sole purpose to bring you to your senses. I hoped to find you reasonable; but, depend upon it, I will carry my point."

"No, Mother, you will not," Anne replied steadily.

"Yes, Anne, I will, for your father's will was highly specific when it comes to your marriage. You have only two choices: marry your cousin Fitzwilliam, or marry a man of my choosing. If you do not, you lose everything; your dowry, Rosings Park, the house in London, everything."

The entire party looked at Lady Catherine, with her eyes glinting as she smiled like an evil Cheshire cat who had just caught her prey. Lady Catherine knew how much Anne loved Rosings Park. Although her daughter talked big now, Lady Catherine understood that when it came right down to it Anne would do almost anything rather than end up on the streets, even marry someone she did not love.

Anne stood shocked; she did not know what to say. She had anticipated the possibility of losing Rosings Park, but she had not thought she would lose her dowry. In fact, she had planned on using it to set up house with Richard. The interest on fifty thousand pounds was a considerable sum, and she anticipated that the two of them could live quite comfortably for their entire lives. She had even hoped her mother would approve so far as to let them live at the London house since she never used it. Anne was not sure she was prepared to live the life of an officer's wife, on an officer's pay. She hesitated, and Lady Catherine knew she had won.

Finally, when silence had fallen between mother and daughter, Lord Matlock stepped in. "Now, let us all calm down and think this through rationally. I am sure there must be a way that Anne can marry for love, and you, Catherine, can be happy with her choice." He smiled lovingly at his niece, whose instant relief spread across her face. "Come, let us take a few days to enjoy Christmas together, and as soon as it is over I will dedicate myself to assisting the two of you in sorting this out. The first thing I will do is send to London for Sir Lewis's will. Let us read the article and see if what you say, Catherine, is spelled out as you say it is. Perhaps you misunderstood."

"Misunderstood? Harrumph! I highly doubt it. I have read his will a hundred times over, making sure I understood it perfectly. We could have all been saved this trouble if Fitzwilliam had just married Anne as he was supposed to."

"Aunt, Anne and I decided long ago that

we had no intention of marrying. We do not love one another as a husband and wife ought. I love Elizabeth, and I believe Anne loves another."

"You cannot possibly mean Richard! I will not stand for it. I do not care that she kissed the fool; we shall all forget about it. No, Anne will have a proper coming out and find a husband in London. For heaven's sake, I never dreamt she needed a coming out or she would have had it years ago. This is all your fault." Lady Catherine waved her hand at Darcy. "Her marriage had been planned from her infancy until that strumpet came along and lured you away."

"Lady Catherine, you will desist insulting my wife or you will be confined to your room for the duration of your visit."

Anne and Richard had been offering one another telling looks. Anne was encouraging him to speak up, which he finally did as Lady Catherine closed her mouth after Fitzwilliam's rebuke.

"Aunt Catherine, I assure you there is someone who knows and loves Anne, even though she never had a coming out."

"Oh, really? And who might that be?"

"Me. I love Anne."

Lady Catherine cackled like a rabid hen, "Oh, that is rich! A military officer seeking the hand of one of England's brightest gems."

Lord Matlock bristled at his sister's response. "Catherine, I bid you watch your tongue. That is my son you are talking about."

"Your son, perhaps, but not your heir. He is a lowly second son with no chance of inheriting. James and Roslynd already have two sons that are in line ahead of him. Nothing could persuade me to allow Anne to marry him. Heaven forbid the shades of Rosings be thus polluted. No, Anne will marry an eldest son with a title, or I shall forbid her to marry."

"You cannot forbid her to marry. To deny her such joy is a selfish act, and I will not allow it. What care you for a title? You planned on marrying her to Fitzwilliam for years, and he does not have a title. Surely such things can mean nothing to you."

"Not allow it? What say have you in the matter?" Lady Catherine ignored his reference to titles; she felt she need not explain herself.

"I am the patriarch of this family, and I will not allow you to do anything that will hurt any member of it." Before she could respond again, Lord Matlock turned and addressed Fitzwilliam. "Take me to your study. I need ink and paper to begin my own inquiries into Sir Lewis's will."

"You shall do no such thing," Lady Catherine yelled. "What right do you have to go meddling in my husband's affairs?"

"I am not meddling, Catherine, I am protecting the rights and interests of your daughter. I am convinced any father who loved his daughter as Lewis did would be happy that another family member is looking out for her. I am confident we will get to the bottom of this. In the meantime, all of you are to remain here. No one, and I mean no one," he looked directly at Anne, "is to leave Pemberley until we have some answers. Now, sister, you go to your room while I write my letters. I will come up to speak with you before supper."

Lady Catherine began to object, but decided to hold her tongue when she saw her brother's angry expression. It was rare James Fitzwilliam, Earl of Matlock, ever angered, but those who had seen him in such a state knew to avoid it a second time.

Lord Matlock, James, Richard, and Fitzwilliam all hastened to Fitzwilliam's study. Anne watched them depart, eager to know what they would do. Richard gave her a look she which understood to mean he would advocate their right to marry.

Richard could no longer hold his tongue as they entered Fitzwilliam's study. "Insufferable presumption! Is she really so unfeeling as to deny Anne her chance at happiness all because of a pedigree?"

Lord Matlock looked at his son. "Yes, she is. She denied herself love in exchange for wealth and comfort; why should she not do the same to her daughter?"

"She may very well destroy her own happiness, but I refuse to let her to ruin Anne's. Hell, if she destroys Anne's happiness, she destroys mine, too. Father, I love Anne. I have for many years now. You must help us find a way to marry or we will elope. We have already discussed it. We would rather face the censure of society and our family than live our lives apart."

"Now, now, let us not be so hasty. Am I to presume the two of you have come to a formal understanding?" Lord Matlock asked his son.

"Yes, we have. We were going to tell everyone on Christmas Day. Father, I love her, and she loves me. Please, I cannot lose her. We must figure this out."

"Very well, we shall. I just needed to know how far I should fight Catherine on this. I would hate to take her to task over it if the two of you were not sincere. If you are serious, then I will not let up until the two of you are married." Lord Matlock looked sternly at his son. "Properly married! I will not hear of my son eloping at Gretna Green. Am I understood?"

"Yes, I understand you perfectly, and I have no objection so long as we get to marry." Richard became very serious as he offered his father his heartfelt thanks.

Lord Matlock gave his son an encouraging smile and sat at Fitzwilliam's desk. He drafted letters to everyone he considered useful in their present situation: the steward of Rosings Park, Sir Lewis de Bourgh's solicitor, his own solicitor, and his own steward.

"There, it is done. Fitzwilliam, would you have your man send these letters to the express post in Lambton?"

Fitzwilliam called immediately for the

butler. Handing the man the letters and some coins, he gave instructions which the man followed at once.

Once the door closed behind the butler, Lord Matlock breathed a sigh of release and said, "I know it is late and only a day from the beginning of the Christmas festivities, but perhaps the letters can be delivered tomorrow and we may have some answers by the beginning of next week."

No one answered him; there was nothing else to do but wait.

# Chapter 13

The past week had been spent in constant movement. Hardly a dull moment was to be had at Pemberley. The entire party, except Lady Catherine, had found entertainment to enjoy.

Fitzwilliam saw to it that sleigh rides were available daily, and the household staff made sure to keep roaring fires in the grates. The children spent much of their time running in and out of the manor all day, making snowmen, snow angels, and getting thoroughly wet and dirty as children do.

Although the week had begun with constant bickering amongst the houseguests and the addition of Lady Catherine had put everyone on edge, it was all turning out well enough. Perhaps everyone remembered the reason for the season, and was determined to get along for at least two days. Elizabeth could hope.

Fitzwilliam and Elizabeth were attempting their first melding of Christmas traditions, and with so many in attendance it would be amusing to see how it would turn out. Everyone had an opinion about how the festivities should proceed, and few were keeping their opinions to themselves.

Christmas Eve supper was a light repast. All day the family had been nibbling on various treats that Mrs. Lacroix had provided, and hardly anyone had any appetite at all. After supper there was no separation of the men to the library, but rather everyone met in the drawing room for the commencement of the evening's festivities.

"My dear family," Fitzwilliam addressed everyone as they took their seats around the room, "I cannot tell you how blessed we are to all be gathered here in the warmth of Pemberley during this beautiful but cold Christmas season."

"Hear, hear!" resounded around the room as everyone agreed.

Elizabeth walked to the little table near the fireplace where the Yule log was nestled and picked it up. She respectfully carried it to Fitzwilliam, who took it in his hands and addressed the party again. "Please join me as I say a prayer over this Yule log for a bountiful year to come."

Fitzwilliam bowed his head as Elizabeth linked her arm through his. The rest of the room joined them and listened as Fitzwilliam offered a heartfelt and wonderful prayer for the health and safety of everyone in the room, their household, the manor, the crops, the livestock, and the tenants. Everyone was blessed, no one was forgotten, and when he completed his prayer Elizabeth had to wipe a tear from her cheek as he placed the log in the center of the fireplace and lit it.

Turning to his uncle, Fitzwilliam asked, "Uncle, will you start us off on a round of toasts?" A few servants had been standing around the room with trays of wine and cider. At his request, the drinks were served to every member of the party.

"I would be honoured, my boy," Lord Matlock replied as he stood and joined Fitzwilliam near the fire.

Elizabeth resumed her seat near her mother just in time to hear her grumbling to her father. "Why should he ask Lord Matlock over you? You are his father-in-law; it is not as if his own father is here to ask. It should be you making the toast." She cringed at her mother's base remarks. She was, of course technically correct; however, Lord Matlock had stood in as Fitzwilliam's surrogate father for the past several years. Her mother had no right to question Fitzwilliam's choice.

Lady Catherine heard the remark and could not pass up the opportunity to slight the Bennet family. "My nephew, of course, understands the distinction of rank. I am sure that is why he has asked his uncle, the Earl, to offer the first toast."

Mrs. Bennet was visibly angered at Lady Catherine's remarks, and Elizabeth feared she or Fitzwilliam would have to step between the two to break up an argument. Mr. Bennet slightly raised his hand to stop his wife's censure of her ladyship's comment. He leaned close to his wife's ear and whispered to her.

No one knew what was said, but Mrs. Bennet's face softened and then she patted Mr. Bennet's knee, as she did when she most heartily agreed with him. Elizabeth could only assume he had told her no one cared what Lady Catherine said, so it was not worth arguing with her. Perhaps he even mentioned it was his suggestion that Lord Matlock make the toast out of respect to his position. The statement would have been at least *mostly* true.

Long before this evening had taken place, Elizabeth had spoken to her father and explained that Fitzwilliam was going to ask Lord Matlock to offer the first toast after the Yule log had been lit. Her father well understood and was not offended in any way. Though he was the only living patriarch to the couple and well within his right to demand he be the first to offer a toast, he understood Lord Matlock was as close to Fitzwilliam's father as another could be. The man did outrank him, and allowing him to offer the toast would likely silence Lady Catherine, which was something everyone longed for.

It worked, almost.

With Lord Matlock's toast complete, Mr. Bennet and Fitzwilliam took the opportunity to offer toasts of their own, as did James, Richard, and Charles. Elizabeth was exceedingly pleased with the evening; everyone was in a most amiable mood.

Looking at the children sitting on the floor next to the Christmas tree, Elizabeth pondered the possibility that next year she may very well be expecting, or even have her own child to enjoy the season with. Nothing would bring her more joy than to bless Pemberley with the pitter-patter of little feet.

Elizabeth and Fitzwilliam had frequently spoken about their future plans for the expansion of their family. They both looked upon the day with eager anticipation and delight.

Roslynd stood while Elizabeth was still admiring the children. "Come, children, it is very late. We must get you to bed so that you can enjoy all of tomorrow's activities."

"Oh, Mother, must we? I want to stay up and have some more cider," James protested, but he stood obediently.

"Yes, you must. Come, follow me."

"Hugs first! We must have our hugs," Evelyn declared.

The three young children took their time going around the room giving everyone a bedtime hug. They barely hesitated at Lady Catherine, looking at her cold face before quickly wrapping their arms around her. She patted their heads with the tips of her fingers, acting as if they had the plague, but still she accepted their sweet tokens of love and affection. By the time they finally finished, they were testing their mother's patience.

"Jane, when you have children, do make sure they are as adorable as those three," Mrs. Bennet began. "Lizzy, I do hope your children will be attractive as well, but if they are anything like you I doubt they will be. You were always one to run around, going hither and thither. Why, you were always getting so much mud on your stockings that I never could keep you presentable. You always had a scraped knee or torn dress, and heaven forbid your hair stayed in place longer than half an hour."

"Yes, well ... Darcy, what is the plan for tomorrow?" Mr. Bennet tried to interrupt his wife's criticism which was obviously upsetting to his second daughter and her husband. Looking towards Lady Catherine's malicious grin, he feared his wife was offering the woman additional fodder against his most beloved daughter.

"Oh yes, my dear Mr. Darcy, what is the plan for tomorrow?" It appeared as if his wife's attention had been at least momentarily redirected from her previous topic.

"I think we will begin the morning with the Christmas breakfast, then we will all gather with the Pemberley tenants and staff, and finally we will open our gifts. In the afternoon, I have a surprise for everyone."

"A surprise," Mrs. Bennet screeched as a murmur of excitement spread around the room.

"Fitzwilliam, have you planned what we did last year?" Georgiana timidly asked.

He pressed his finger to his lips as if it was a secret and winked at her. She giggled with excitement then exclaimed to Mary and Kitty sitting near her, "Oh, what fun we shall have. I promise you will *love* it." Already the girls were excited, begging Georgiana to give them any hint she could about the surprise.

Pressing her lips together tightly in a show of *not saying a word*, she continued to tease them. The three girls loved every minute of it.

"Oh, you cruel man, why do you tease us so? I never could enjoy a surprise. You had better tell us now," Mrs. Bennet chided.

"No, you must wait until tomorrow. I promise it will be well worth it."

The evening was waning and already most of the party had dispersed. Georgiana, Mary, and Kitty were in Georgiana's rooms, where giggling and female chatter could be heard well into the night. Mr. and Mrs. Bennet sat in the corner near the fire. Mrs. Bennet dozed while her husband read one of the many books he had found of interest in the Pemberley library.

Fitzwilliam and Elizabeth sat near Lord and Lady Matlock, and though Elizabeth was just becoming acquainted with her new family, she was quickly coming to love Fitzwilliam's favourite uncle and aunt. Roslynd returned after the children were in bed, but she soon became frustrated with Lady Catherine's views on the proper methods to raise children. She and James soon retired to their rooms for the evening, leaving Lady Catherine to turn her attention to the others.

Anne and Richard had settled in the farthest corner of the room, out of Lady Catherine's direct line of sight. Anne had hoped they would be forgotten, but as soon as James and Roslynd had left, her mother no longer had occupation and turned her attention to her daughter. "Anne, you will come to me at once," Lady Catherine demanded.

Anne rolled her eyes at Richard, indicating her derision for her mother, but she stood and walked to her side. Sitting near her, Anne was instantly subjected to a barrage of her mother's demands. "Anne, I am most seriously displeased. Under the present circumstances, you deserve no such attention, but I will tell you this, I am willing to overlook all of your indiscretions if you leave with me and come to London. There we will find you a *proper* husband."

"No, Mother, I will not. I intend to marry Richard, and nothing you say will ever change my mind."

"What has gotten into you? You spend a few days in the presence of *that woman*," she pointed at Elizabeth, "and now I am subjected to utter nonsense. I will not hear any more of it. You will do your duty to your family, and that is the end of it."

Fitzwilliam stood, ready to defend Elizabeth against his coarse aunt, but Lord Matlock beat him to it.

"Catherine, that is enough!" Lord Matlock commanded. The attention of the entire room had been caught when his sister's voice was heard raised against Anne. Now they all sat straighter and hung on his every word. "We know not what Anne's duty is at this point, and until our stewards and solicitors arrive with Lewis's will and the proper documents, you will cease mentioning any of it. In addition, I will not hear another remark against Elizabeth. She is as much of a member of this family as you and I."

"How dare you presume I do not know what my husband's will states? When everyone you have called to Pemberley rally around and confirm what I have told you, I will demand an apology from you, James." Lady Catherine's voice was seething with anger against her brother. "Once I have it, I will take my daughter and we will leave this place, at which time she will marry whom I deem appropriate."

"No, Mother, I will not go with you." Anne ran from the room; Richard followed her.

"Then you will be disowned, left penniless, and at the mercy of these relations who seem to think your father's wishes mean nothing," Lady Catherine yelled after the retreating figure of her daughter.

Richard caught up with Anne at the top of the stairs. Reaching out, he caught her arm and pulled her to him.

"Why? Why must my mother be so vicious?" Anne sobbed into Richard's chest.

"Shhh, do not cry. My father has assured me he will find a way for us to marry."

"How? If my mother is right, then my father has forced me into a life of misery. A life married to someone my mother chooses. A life without love."

Richard placed his hand under Anne's chin and lifted her face so he could look directly into her eyes while he spoke. "If my father is not successful, then we will do what we must. Nothing will keep us apart."

"Promise?"

"I promise."

Richard reached into his pocket and then held his hand above Anne's head. As she looked up to see what he was doing, he caught her lips in a passionate kiss. Pulling away, he declared, "I think I like Elizabeth's Christmas decorations. They have proved extremely useful."

The tears in Anne's eyes disappeared as a beautiful smile lit up her face. She reached for Richard's hand and took the mistletoe from him; then, holding it over his head, she kissed him again.

## Chapter 14

Christmas morning was a flurry of activity. The Fitzwilliam children were running around, giggling and laughing merrily about everything they saw. The tree that had been empty yesterday was now filled with presents, and they could hardly wait to open them.

The boisterous nature of the children had set Mrs. Bennet's nerves a flutter just days before, but today she matched their energy and smiled at the beautiful sight of happy children.

"Jane, Lizzy, aren't the children just delightful? Why, just look at them. Nothing but smiles from all three. Oh, how I have missed the excitement of small children on Christmas morning."

"Yes, Mamma," Jane answered and then cast a look at her sister.

Elizabeth looked back at her and rolled her eyes with derision. Jane responded with a shrug of her shoulders. Elizabeth was happy her mother had chosen to enjoy the children rather than censure them, for she doubted she could handle two censuring matrons. Lady Catherine was quite enough.

"Lord James, Lady Roslynd, I am sure you can imagine a lady of my age and station in life prefers not to be awakened by the screams of unruly children at God only knows what hour it is," Lady Catherine ranted as she entered the drawing room.

James looked towards his aunt and responded without a care of whether he offended her or not. "Aunt Catherine, today is Christmas and the children are excited. I care not that their joyful exclamations woke you up. You will just have to deal with it."

"Well, I never—"

She was cut off by the high-pitched squeals of the children as their grandparents entered the room. "Grandpapa, Grandmamma, look!" Evelyn exclaimed as she threw her arms around their legs and pointed to the tree. "We have presents, lots of them. May we open them?"

Lady Matlock bent down and lifted little

Richard into her arms as he toddled up behind his sister. "Not yet. We must eat breakfast and give gifts to the tenants, then when we return this afternoon we will open our own presents. Remember, children, duty always comes before pleasure, but let me tell you a little secret." She sat upon the settee with Richard on her lap and leaned towards James and Evelyn, who came to stand next to her. "It will be lots of fun to hand out presents and play with Cousin Fitzwilliam's tenants and their children. I dare you to keep a bigger smile on your face than the children you see today."

"That will be easy," responded James. "I am so happy I could burst."

"You could, could you?" Lady Matlock reached out and tickled his tummy. He doubled over laughing. When he stood, he reached into his pocket and pulled out a piece of mistletoe. He held it over his grandmother's head and quickly leaned in to kiss her cheek.

"I kissed you, Grandmamma."

"Yes you did, dearest. What do you have there in your hand?"

"It is mistletoe. I found it on the floor by the staircase. I know what to do with it because I saw Uncle Richard hold it over his head when he kissed Cousin Anne yesterday."

"Oh? And where did you see him kiss her?"

"On the lips."

Lady Matlock tried to stifle a smile as Richard and Anne entered the room arm in arm. She looked directly at her son as she further questioned her grandson. "And where were Uncle Richard and Cousin Anne when you saw them kissing on the lips?"

Anne's face was overcome with a brilliant shade of red, but Richard took his mother's questioning of his nephew in stride. He was not worried that the boy had witnessed their encounter, for he had it on reliable authority from his brother that the boy had stumbled on a few amorous encounters of his parents in the past. Such were the woes of children. No, he was more worried about his aunt.

Before James could respond, Lady Catherine was standing and addressing the couple herself. "Kissing! Am I to understand young James caught the two of you kissing? It is bad enough that the rest of us had to witness such a display, but in front of the children? Consider if you will that it will be hard enough to hush up the first kiss. It will be impossible to protect Anne's honour if you insist on repeating it, and in front of the children."

Anne was still regaining her composure and was not up to the task of confrontation with her mother, but Richard was ready for her. "Yes, it appears he did see us, though I assure you we thought we were alone."

"Alone! Why, that is even worse. Anne, I forbid you from being alone with him." Lady Catherine reached her hand to Anne and tried to pull her away from Richard, but by now she had recovered.

"No, Mother. I am of age, and I will be alone with anyone I choose."

"You speak nonsense. Do you not know what it will do to your reputation?"

"There are hardly those who will censure a woman for a few stolen minutes with her fiancé."

"Fiancé? No, I will not allow it. I have already told you that you only had two options for marriage: marry Fitzwilliam or a man of my choosing. As I said before, Richard is a second son without title or fortune. You cannot marry him."

At Lady Catherine's emphatic statement,

she, Anne, and Richard all began yelling at once.

"Catherine, Anne, Richard, that is enough. Today is Christmas, and I demand we hear no more about this issue. You will either remain here and spend today in a joyful manner with the rest of us or return to your respective rooms and not come out until tomorrow." Lord Matlock felt as if he was scolding little children rather than three mature adults.

"Yes, Father," responded Richard in unison with Anne's "Yes, Uncle."

Lady Catherine said not a word; instead, she thundered from the room and up the stairs. Despite the distance of her rooms from the drawing room, a few moments later the entire party heard her door slam. She was not seen for the remainder of the day. All of the trays Elizabeth had sent to her were returned without being touched.

The poor attitude of Lady Catherine had no bearing on the rest of the party. As soon as the children returned to their exuberant natures, everyone else joined in and celebrated the day's festivities.

The Christmas breakfast was a glorious affair, and when it ended everyone walked to the ballroom where the Pemberley tenants and staff gathered each year to be addressed by Mr. Darcy.

The entire party entered the room with Fitzwilliam and Elizabeth in the lead carrying an urn of the Yule log ashes.

Mr. Darcy addressed all in attendance, offering a prayer for the manor, the Darcy family, the crops, and finally the tenants, the staff, and their families. A handful of the ashes was spread over a box full of Pemberley soil, and the remaining ashes in the urn were handed to the steward with instructions to spread them over all of the fields after the winter frost had receded and before the new year's seed was planted.

The entire assembly rejoiced when Mr. Darcy introduced Elizabeth to them, and they all bowed and curtsied when Elizabeth addressed them.

By the time the gathering ended, the generosity of Mr. Darcy was again to be praised, and all of the tenants and those who relied upon Pemberley rejoiced that Mr. Darcy had found a bride worthy of him. They were overjoyed that Mr. Darcy had finally married, and that Pemberley had a proper mistress. It boded well for the continued prosperity of the estate. The only event that could exceed their joy in the marriage would be the announcement when an heir was born.

Normally the crowd would disperse and all would return to their homes at the conclusion of the Christmas gathering, but not today. A line began to form near Fitzwilliam and Elizabeth, and it quickly became clear that everyone wanted to meet the new mistress in person. The rest of the family returned to the drawing room and waited for more than two hours while Fitzwilliam introduced his bride to everyone who relied on Pemberley for their living. Elizabeth was overwhelmed by their outpouring of congratulations and began to feel that it really meant something to be the Mistress of Pemberley.

"I am sorry we took so long. I hope you are all prepared to open presents," Fitzwilliam said as he walked into the room with Elizabeth on his arm.

The children shouted with delight and raced to the tree, kneeling in front of the piled gifts. James rushed to the side of his children. He understood that after two hours of waiting it took every ounce of their self-control not to start grabbing at the presents.

"Fitzwilliam, if it is all right with you, I will allow the children to hand out the presents."

"Very well, James, if they want to."

James addressed his three young children. "What do you say, would you three like to hand out the presents?"

"Yes!" all three shouted in unison as they bounced on their knees with excitement.

James reached under the tree for each present, calling off the names of the recipients as he handed the gifts, in turn, to his three children to distribute.

The Bennets were surprised when they received presents from the Darcys. Kitty mentioned it first. "Lizzy, I thought you said our presents were sent to Longbourn."

"They were. You have Fitzwilliam to thank for these. The day you arrived he was thoughtful enough to send a man all the way to Longbourn to collect the gifts we had sent there. He returned just last night."

"Oh, Mr. Darcy, how good you are to us," cooed Mrs. Bennet. "Is he not a good son-in-law, Mr. Bennet?"

"Yes, I dare say he is."

When all of the gifts from under the tree were handed out, James and the children settled near Roslynd and the festivities began.

Everyone took turns opening their gifts while the rest of the family looked on with delight. It was a truly enjoyable process, and in the end all were satisfied with their gifts, none more so than the children. James had received a gift worthy of a man, a pocket knife his father promised he would teach him to use. Evelyn held five new outfits for her doll, Lizzy, and Richard had a pile of painted wooden blocks he had already stacked and knocked over four times. He shouted with glee each time they crashed to the ground.

Georgiana and Mary compared their new sheet music while Kitty tried on her new bonnet. All three of them then talked about how beautiful their dresses would be when they had the opportunity to properly trim them with the new lace and ornaments they had received. No three girls could be happier.

Mr. Bennet was pleased with his new books, many of them first editions he had never dreamed of owning, and Mrs. Bennet admired the superior quality of the French tapestry she was positive Mr. Darcy had spent a fortune on.

Elizabeth's gift from her husband was the most grand of all. Fitzwilliam had bought her a jewellery set worthy of a queen. The ruby and diamond necklace, bracelet, and ring perfectly matched the red gown she wore, and everyone begged her to try them on. She hesitated, terrified to wear something so valuable.

Fitzwilliam, however, was dying to see her in them, and rather than watch her hesitate, he took the box from her and gently removed the necklace. Standing behind her, he draped the necklace around her neck and closed the clasp. Everyone looked on in awe as the cold stones lying against her creamy flesh sparkled in the sunlight from the window.

When Mrs. Bennet realized Jane had not been given a gift as grand as Elizabeth's, she patted Jane's hand and said, "Do not worry, my dear, Mr. Bingley is not so rich as Mr. Darcy, and perhaps he does not recognize the importance of offering his wife a glorious gift at Christmas."

Jane was tired of her mother constantly

comparing her two sons-in-law and, despite the fact no one wanted any more bickering at Christmas, she could not allow her mother to believe her husband did not love her so much as Fitzwilliam loved Elizabeth simply because she did not have a tangible gift in her hands.

"Mother, I would appreciate it if you would not say such things. Charles has given me exactly what I wanted for Christmas. Just because I did not receive a gift under the tree that I could unwrap with the rest of you does not mean I did not receive something grand."

Mrs. Bennet's eyes rose in a questioning look. "Really, Jane, you received what you wanted? What did he give you? Do tell."

Elizabeth looked at Jane. She knew her sister would prefer to tell their mother in private about her gift rather than face her shock and distress in company. Nonetheless, Jane plunged forward. "Mother, Father." Jane took a deep breath and grasped Charles's hand for support as the eyes of everyone in the room turned to her. "Charles and I have decided to give up our lease at Netherfield and have taken a house here in the north, near Elizabeth and Fitzwilliam.

When we stopped to take in the view on our way here, we were looking down upon our new home. It is but seven miles from here."

Mrs. Bennet sat in shock for a full five minutes, unable to say anything. Mr. Bennet offered his sincere congratulations. He had known Jane and Charles would not stay in the neighborhood long, not with the amount of time his wife had already spent at their home in their first two weeks of their marriage. To own the truth, he did not blame them. He would have done the same.

When finally Mrs. Bennet had regained her speech, she was subdued. She congratulated Jane and Charles, but then sat in silence for close to twenty minutes. Everyone could tell she was saddened to lose another daughter. Mr. Bennet sat near her and repeatedly patted her hand as his way of offering her comfort, which she accepted. He knew his wife well; her heart was truly breaking. To have three daughters married was a fulfillment of her life's desire and brought her considerable joy, but never had she imagined that they would all move to distant parts of the country where she would hardly see them again.

Looking out the window, Georgiana noticed the position of the sun in the afternoon sky. "Fitzwilliam, the afternoon is beginning to wane. Do you still plan on the surprise?"

The Fitzwilliam children quickly lunged to their feet and begged his positive response. "Yes, we must, you promised."

Looking at the clock on the mantle, he exclaimed, "Is that actually the time? We had better get started or we will not have enough light." Then, turning to address the room, specifically the Fitzwilliam children and Bennet sisters, he exclaimed. "Everyone needs to hurry and dress in the warmest clothes you have. Make sure they are not your best clothes, for they are sure to get dirty. Then join me in the foyer in ten minutes."

The children begged to know what was going on, their excitement overflowing every bit as much as it had earlier in the day as they anticipated opening their gifts. Their parents ushered them out of the room to prepare, and very soon the entire party was standing in the foyer dressed in heavy coats, hats, gloves, and scarves.

The butler opened the door and everyone followed Fitzwilliam outside. He led everyone across the lawn and up the hill to a little grove of trees. There, propped against the trees, were five sleds.

Georgiana was the only one of the party who knew what a sled was. Fitzwilliam offered a brief description of the object that originated from Scotland, and then demonstrated how it should be used. The children screamed with delight when he laid on his stomach and flew down the hill. As he reached the bottom and began his trek back to the top, they begged him for the chance to try.

Fitzwilliam assured them that everyone would get a chance, and when he reached the top again he situated James on his own sled and sent him squealing with delight down the hill while his sister begged to go next. Roslynd worried that Evelyn and Richard were too small to sled alone, so her husband took up the next sled and set his two youngest children on his lap. The three made it safely to the bottom of the hill, rolling off the sled in a heap of laughter.

The Bennet sisters and Georgiana took their turns together in a race to the bottom, but Kitty never made it. She fell off about halfway down. At first everyone was afraid she had been hurt, but when she rolled a few times and then sat up laughing, they joined her in the merriment.

Everyone, young and old, took their turn on the sleds and enjoyed every moment of it.

As the sun slipped from the sky, the entire party walked back to the manor. Everyone's clothing was dirty and wet, but Fitzwilliam had thought of everything. While their party was out playing and having fun, the Pemberley staff were in dashing here and there in a frenzy to heat enough water for eighteen warm baths.

The dinner bell rang just as Lord and Lady Matlock, the last to come down, entered the drawing room where the rest of the party was assembled.

The room was a buzz of excitement as everyone talked about the sledding excursion. Young James was the most boisterous, demanding to know if everyone had seen how fast he had gone. The children begged to go sledding again tomorrow while their parents tried to appease them with vague answers of "we will see."

Now that everyone was assembled, a servant entered and announced dinner.

Fitzwilliam offered Elizabeth his arm and invited everyone to join him in the dining room for a Christmas feast. When they entered, everyone looked around in awe. The room was drenched in candlelight and festive evergreen decorations that Elizabeth and Mrs. Reynolds had spent hours preparing. The table was laden with a feast the likes of which few had ever beheld. Rather than have the servants carry out dish after dish, Elizabeth had instructed the food to be placed in the center of the table. Seeing it all laid out in front of them was a spectacular sight.

The entire party found their places around the table and took their seats. Fitzwilliam then stood and offered a marvelous speech of hope and gratitude. He closed with a prayer to the Almighty God, and then invited everyone to partake.

Instantly the room was thrown into a frenzy of serving spoons clanking against the finest tableware at Pemberley. Conversation and activity were everywhere. Elizabeth paused and looked over the crowd in front of her. Not a cross word came from anyone. Everyone was happy and enjoying one another's company. She could not be more thankful or ask for anything more.

Dinner lasted for more than an hour before the dishes were removed and dessert laid before them.

"Grandpapa, look! It is Christmas pudding. I knew we were going to have it. Lizzy told me."

"She did, did she?" Lord Matlock questioned his grandson.

"Yes, she did. I was there, too," Little Evelyn added. "We told her she had to or you would be cross all year." She giggled as she imparted her secret.

Lord Matlock laughed a loud and boisterous laugh as he dug in with his spoon and filled his dish.

The entire party wondered whether they were too full to eat another bite, but in the end they found room and ate every last spoonful.

Finally, Christmas dinner was over and the entire party returned to the drawing room. As everyone exited the room, Mrs. Bennet called Elizabeth to her side. "Lizzy, my dear, you are to be commended. The meal was delicious. You offered your guests a stunning variety of dishes that was sure to satisfy even the most diverse of palates. I must say it was better than I ever imagined. I cannot think of a single dish that was missed. Congratulations on such a successful dinner."

Mrs. Bennet kissed her daughter's cheek and was just turning to follow her husband when Elizabeth caught her arm and responded, "Thank you, Mother. Your approval means a great deal to me since you are such a proficient hostess."

Mrs. Bennet patted Elizabeth's hand on her arm. "I think you are in a fair way to becoming a proficient hostess yourself. There are not many who could host a celebration of such magnitude in a new place, and with such varied preferences to cater to, with so much success. Not to mention that so many were surprise guests." Mrs. Bennet winked at Elizabeth, knowing she was one of those surprise guests.

"Mamma, if we have time before you leave, I would like to ask you a few questions about your methods of overseeing the household. Now that I have my own home and have been mistress for a few weeks, I am sure there are a few things I could use your advice on."

"I would like that, Lizzy." Mrs. Bennet beamed at her daughter, happy that Elizabeth would seek any knowledge and advice from her.

# Chapter 15

Lady Catherine had not left her room since entering it on Christmas morning, but now that the day of festivities was passed, she was bound and determined to make her sentiments known. From the moment she came downstairs, she was threatening and obstinate, making demands at the top of her voice for the entire house to hear.

No one could convince her to act reasonably, and finally gave up after an hour of trying. The rest of the morning and much of the afternoon, all that could be heard through the rooms and halls of Pemberley were Lady Catherine's threats.

James and Lord Matlock had escaped the house by begging the use of the sleds from Fitzwilliam. The two fled with all three children and were currently enjoying another adventure.

Georgiana, Mary, and Kitty had been tucked in the corner at the little table all day. There were gowns, wraps, and bonnets strewn everywhere as the girls worked tirelessly to trim them anew.

Lady Matlock and Roslynd had taken on the difficult task of sitting with Lady Catherine, but Elizabeth, unable to take much more of her ladyships demands, retreated to the Orangery for a moment of peace and solitude. When she arrived she soon discovered she was not alone. Richard and Anne were also there discussing their plans to elope to Gretna Green. Elizabeth feared what she was overhearing.

Stepping around the corner and into their view, she addressed them. "I apologize, but I could not help overhearing your conversation. I promise you I was not trying to eavesdrop; I was merely trying to escape to somewhere private."

"Yes, we had the same inclination," Richard said.

"This Orangery, so far, is my favorite place at Pemberley. Fitzwilliam and I often take walks here and talk. I understand how the two of you have also found it a convenient place for private discussions."

"How much did you hear?" Anne questioned.

"Enough to understand that very soon the two of you plan to elope to Gretna Green."

Richard and Anne looked at Elizabeth but did not say a word. She continued, "I will not stop you, but let me advise you against it. Fitzwilliam and I have talked at length, and we are confident there will be a positive resolution to your mother's objections. Lord Matlock has assured us he will not rest until the two of you are able to marry with your family nearby, rejoicing in your union. Do not go off in secret and cause distress to so many when you have a chance at genuine happiness. In the end, eloping will bring you pain even if it grants you temporary happiness. Please, give everyone some time to determine on the state of Anne's affairs. For heaven's sake, the solicitors have not even arrived with the will yet."

Anne looked up at Richard, who nodded to her. "Very well. We will not run away before the new year, but if the solicitors do not arrive and find some solution soon, we are determined to elope. I cannot fight my mother forever, and as long as we are unmarried she will continue to run my life.

I would rather marry and know I have lost everything except my husband then wonder what method she will next employ to secure her position."

Elizabeth understood their situation, perhaps even agreed with them deep down, but as a member of the family she could not stand by while they planned to elope without offering advice against it. Eloping was temporary happiness, but once the scandal of the event caught up with the couple, there would be far more harm done than ever imagined.

She turned to leave them to themselves, offering one additional thought to them before she departed. "If I may be so bold, let me suggest another option. If needs be, Fitzwilliam and I will call the Pemberley parson and have him perform your marriage by special license. It will be a union supported by the family, even if your mother does not accept it. No matter what, promise me you will not elope."

Anne thanked Elizabeth for her advice and gave her a hug before she left. No promise had been made, but Richard and Anne felt her kindness and truly appreciated her support.

After Elizabeth retreated from the couple, she sought out Fitzwilliam in his study.

When she entered, he held out his hand to her. She accepted it as she stepped close to him. He slid his chair back from his desk and then pulled her onto his lap. She snuggled into him, her legs draped over his, as he wrapped his arms around her.

"Good afternoon, Mrs. Darcy. What brings you to my study this fine day?" He was teasing her, and she knew it and loved it.

Elizabeth stayed on his lap, sitting up straight as she told him of Anne and Richard's plan to elope and her subsequent offer to let them marry in the Pemberley chapel. He praised her quick thinking and assured her he supported her decision. He professed his belief that none of it would be necessary because everyone was determined to find a solution that allowed Anne to marry for love.

"I hope so. I fervently believe everyone should marry for love," said Elizabeth.

"As do I," answered Fitzwilliam as he kissed her.

The two remained alone in the study for close to an hour, moving only as far as the leather sofa in the corner. They reclined together, enjoying the opportunity to be alone though their house was full of guests.

# Chapter 16

Sunday was no better than the day before. Lady Catherine continued to storm around the manor as if she owned it, making demands of everyone that crossed her path. The more impatient she grew, the more unreasonable her demands became.

Everyone was relieved on Monday when both solicitors and the stewards arrived from London. The men were offered rooms to rest in and meals to warm them. It was not long before all four men came downstairs and were ready to being the business for which they had been summoned to Pemberley.

Lord Matlock thanked them all for coming. Mr. Macintyre, Sir Lewis de Bourgh's attorney, and Mr. Brown, his own solicitor, were both there to provide legal advice. He explained to Mr. Macintyre that they needed to understand Sir Lewis's will as it read regarding his daughter Anne de Bourgh. He further explained that Mr. Brown was there to advise him on his options should he desire as patriarch of the family to petition the will.

Mr. Macintyre looked aghast at Lord Matlock and replied, "Why would you want to petition the will? Sir Lewis provided handsomely for his daughter. I helped him to draft her provisions, and I assure you he was specific in every detail."

"Yes, well, it is that specificity I am concerned about. It is my goal to make sure Anne has a say in the decisions that affect her life most."

"Yes, sir, that was her father's intent as well."

Lord Matlock looked at the man skeptically. "It is my understanding from my sister, Sir Lewis de Bourgh's widow, that Anne does not have a say in those matters that affect her life most significantly; her marriage, for instance."

"Yes she does. Come, let us read the will. Sir Lewis de Bourgh was adamant that Anne should never be forced into a marriage she does not want."

Lord Matlock, James, Richard, and

Fitzwilliam all eyed each other. They were skeptical but hopeful at the same time.

Mr. Macintyre opened his satchel and pulled out a large stack of documents. All of the men listened closely as he read aloud from the pages. They could scarcely believe their ears. Sir Lewis de Bourgh's will detailed the provisions Anne was to receive in a detail none of them ever imagined.

"CATHERINE!" bellowed Lord Matlock through the halls of Pemberley.

Anne came running from the drawing room and looked with concern from her uncle to Richard. Her eyes pleaded for him to tell her what was the matter, but he could not; the shock was still too great.

Fitzwilliam came to the couple's side and assured Anne, "All is well. Uncle will reveal all in due time. Rest assured, the two of you will marry."

Anne's knees went weak with relief. Had Fitzwilliam not been there to catch her, he doubted Richard would have come to his senses in time to perform the service. He supported Anne until she had regained her composure, and then turned her over to

Richard, who had recovered enough to care for her.

Elizabeth approached her husband and asked, "Is all well, Fitzwilliam? Is it true that Richard and Anne are free to marry?"

He nodded his head but would not say more.

Ten minutes later, an exceedingly angry Lord Matlock led his scolded sister into Fitzwilliam's study and called the whole family in to witness. Anne, Lady Matlock, Roslynd, and Elizabeth all entered the room and stood next to the men they loved.

The room was silent until finally Lord Matlock began to speak. "Mr. Macintyre has brought with him a copy of Sir Lewis de Bourgh's will. I must admit, at least for my own part, that it is vastly different from anything I have been led to believe, or even imagined." He looked scathingly at his sister. "Anne, I am sorry to be so blunt, but your mother has lied to you for many years, and I am happy to say you are free to marry the man of your choice without fear of being disinherited." Anne's knuckles where white as she tightly grasped Richard's hand in her own. "I think it best if we have Mr. Macintyre read you the relevant sections of your father's will. I think you will be happy to discover how much your father loved you, my dear."

Anne smiled at her uncle and turned her wondering eyes to Mr. Macintyre.

"The beginning of his Last Will and Testament is all of the usual legal jargon and evidence of witnesses. Let me see, I think this is a good place to start." Mr. Macintyre situated his glasses upon the end of his nose and read aloud a section of the will. Upon conclusion of the section, he looked up from the documents and said, "To make sure that all of the ladies understand, I would like to speak in gentler terms and clarify. This section means that Anne is free to marry anyone she chooses. Her marriage portion is to be £50,000. In addition, upon her marriage she assumes full responsibility, with her husband, of Rosings Park. In addition, if she is still unmarried at the age of eight and twenty, Anne will assume full responsibility for all aspects of Rosings Park—"

"Yes, yes, we all understand what the will says. We are intelligent women." Anne turned her fierce eyes on her mother. "Mother, how could you? You have known all these years what father's will said, and yet you maintained I must marry Fitzwilliam. Not only that, but once he married Elizabeth you continued to make me think it was you who would choose my husband, when all this time it should have been my choice. Richard and I have lost years of happiness because of your cruelty." Anne took a deep breath, her ire rising even more as she considered the attorney's words. "I was supposed to assume full responsibility of Rosings Park more than eight months ago? I would like to understand why you never told me any of this. Why you led me to believe I would be cast away from Rosings Park if I did not marry whom you wanted, when in fact I should already be Mistress of Rosings Park." Then, turning to Mr. Macintyre, she addressed him. "And why have you never told me? I understand that my father's brother was executor of my father's will and should have been the one to tell me, but he has been dead for years. When I came of age, was it not your responsibility to inform me? Your responsibility to ensure my father's will was executed in the absence of my uncle?"

Mr. Macintyre was concerned. She was right, and he had tried to speak to her on several occasions, but her mother had always said she was sick. He had never questioned Lady Catherine or dared to intrude upon Anne under such conditions.

Lord Matlock placed a calming hand on his niece's arm. "Come, Anne, please allow Mr. Macintyre to finish. I think you will be mightily interested in learning what else your father set forth in his will for you."

"What, there is more?" Anne questioned.

Mr. Macintyre continued, his voice a little hesitant, for he did not want to increase the ire of Miss de Bourgh. "Yes, Miss de Bourgh, there is more. Upon your marriage or your eight and twentieth birthday, whichever comes first, you become responsible for the decision of where your mother is to live. She of course has her marriage portion, which was £25,000 and all cumulative interest, but you choose whether she is to remain at Rosings Park, move to the London Townhouse, or the Rosings Dowager House. Your mother loses her marriage settlement of £25,000 and all its cumulated interest due to the financial distress the estate is currently in."

"Financial distress?" Anne questioned. "What do you mean?"

All eyes turned towards Mr. Johnson, the

steward of Rosings Park. "Miss de Bourgh," Mr. Johnson glanced at Lady Catherine with a bit of trepidation and fear as Anne nodded for him to continue, "as of the week before Christmas, all of the financial accounts are drained; in fact, some of them are in arrears. I have been recommending to your mother for the past six months that she should retrench, but she assured me that you would soon marry, which would provide sufficient funds to bring the accounts into balance."

A general cry went up around the room and all eyes went to Lady Catherine, who sat with her arms folded across her chest, a smirk on her face.

"How is that possible? Ever since the death of your late husband's brother, you have had me review the estate ledgers," Fitzwilliam exclaimed.

Lady Catherine rounded on her nephew. "Of course I had you review the ledgers. You were supposed to marry Anne! I had to make sure that you understood the worth of Rosings Park and how wealthy it would make you when combined with your precious Pemberley."

Mr. Johnson feared for his position, but it was time everyone knew the truth. "Her ladyship has instructed me to maintain a separate ledger these past ten years complete. She advises me which transactions are to be withheld from the ledgers you review."

"Catherine, how could you?" Lord Matlock asked his sister in an accusing manner. His tone became harsh as he demanded answers. "What is the current financial state of Rosings Park?" Mr. Johnson began to respond, but Lord Matlock held up his hand to silence him. "Catherine, I asked you a question. You will answer me at once."

Lady Catherine raised dark eyes that seethed with rage and hatred towards her brother. "There is no financial state because all of the money is gone. Every last penny of it. I made sure of that."

"Why? How could you do such a thing?"

"It has been evident to me for years that Anne and Fitzwilliam had mutually decided against marrying. All my well-laid plans were destroyed, just like that; gone with the frivolous concept of *true love*." She practically spat the words from her mouth. "I was denied true love, and Anne's fate shall be the same. If she wants to keep her beloved Rosings Park, then she will do as I say and marry a wealthy man who can restore the estate to its former grandeur."

"Catherine, you were not denied true love. You chose to marry for wealth. No one forced you."

"Of course I was forced. Father made it clear to me that no sensible man would have me, so when sir Lewis de Bourgh approached him with an offer, he accepted him. I was informed that I would marry him, even when I told father that I expected another to ask for my hand. Father didn't agree; he said the man would never ask and demanded that I marry Lewis. Well, I did it. I gave up true love and married Lewis, and for what? Nothing. Even had the other man not asked, I would have been happy to wile away my days as a spinster. In fact, I should have preferred it."

"So you decided that because you were forced into what you consider a miserable life that you would force your daughter into the same? Shame on you! But at least your plan was thwarted. I suppose you never imagined your husband would understand the depth of your manipulative character, did you? Still, it is no excuse for running the estate to ruin."

"Yes, it is. I have immense pleasure sitting here knowing there is nothing you can do to prevent it at this point. Anne must marry a man of fortune or she loses it all." Looking at Anne, she steepled her fingers and tapped them against her pursed lips as she chanted, "Choices, choices, choices."

It was difficult for anyone to comprehend the extent of Lady Catherine's lies and deceit. Lady Matlock could not believe it possible that any woman would injure her daughter, her own flesh and blood, in such a manner. Lord Matlock had trouble pinpointing when the sweet sister he remembered had grown into such a vindictive person. He understood she had changed over the years, but even in his darkest thoughts he never imagined her as vicious as this. Lady Matlock tried to calm her husband with reassuring caresses on his arm, but, to own the truth, she was ready to strike Catherine.

Elizabeth admitted to Fitzwilliam that, at any moment, she expected to wake up from this horrid dream. He was aghast, dismayed, and horrified that Lady Catherine could run the estate into ruin, right under his nose, and he not see it. James and Roslynd did not know what to think.

In a final attempt to raise everyone's ire, Lady Catherine threw one last slight at Richard. "The question is, Richard, does she love you enough to give up Rosings Park and follow you around on your little army assignments, or will she forget all about you and find a man who has the means to provide for her the lifestyle to which she is accustomed?"

The question hung in the air like a pendulum until Anne answered it. "I choose to marry Richard, and it matters not whether he has a fortune. We will use my dowry and your marriage settlement to restore Rosings Park, even if it takes every penny of it." Despite her declaration, the excitement Anne had felt at being able to marry as she pleased was wholly overshadowed by the gloom of losing Rosings Park.

The room was silent until finally Lord Matlock chose to break up the gathering. "Come, I think we should all leave Anne and Richard. I believe they will have much to talk about." It had been a long day, and everyone had much on their minds as they left the room.

As the door closed behind them Anne turned towards Richard. His expression was clouded, and Anne was unable to determine his feelings. It was apparent to him that Anne needed a man who could help her run an estate, not a man of the army.

The significance of everything they had been told was beginning to sink in, and before Anne could say a word, Richard addressed her. "Anne, I think you should take a day to think through all you have learned. From the sound of it, Rosings Park will need a rather large infusion of money. I do not want you to have to use your dowry to save your home."

"Richard, what are you saying?" Anne questioned with eyes full of fear.

"I am saying you have been out in society so little. What if there is another man you could love? A man with enough money to help you save Rosings Park."

"There is no one else I could love; I love only you."

"That is not true. So many people find love, then lose it, just to find love again. I think you owe it to yourself to go to London and meet other men."

"No, I will not. If you will not marry me,

then I will return to Rosings Park on my own. I will marry no one but you."

"Do not be that way, Anne. You should at least think about it. We will speak again tomorrow, but for now please consider what I have said. It certainly would make your life easier if you found a wealthy man to love. Consider, I am not ready to give up my life as a man of the army, and you should not be asked to give up the lifestyle in which you have been raised."

"Richard, I cannot believe what you are saying. I am not asking you to give up your position, nor am I proposing that I give up mine. We have only just learned the facts. Let us both do as you say; let us think about it before we make any decisions."

Richard understood that Anne loved him, but he also understood her devotion to her ancestral home. If he were the heir to Matlock he knew he would do anything to save it. He did not want her to feel obligated to marry him now that she understood the true nature of Rosings Park's financial affairs.

With no more than a kiss on her hand, Richard left Anne standing in the study as tears rolled down her face. Her sobs seemed to follow him through the halls, chasing him all the way to his rooms.

Richard collapsed on the bed without removing his clothes. His mind reeled with a hundred variations of his life; scenarios of joy and sorrow. A few minutes later there was a knock at the door. When he opened it, the butler stood on the other side with a letter in his hand.

"Sir, a letter just came express for you."

"Thank you," Richard said as he took it. He opened the letter as he closed the door with his foot and walked deeper into the room. He was surprised to see it was from his general; there had been no official seal on the envelope, and beyond the polite salutation it contained an extraordinary request.

*Colonel R. Fitzwilliam,*

*I hope you are enjoying the Christmas season with your family in the North.*

*Though Militia deserters no longer fall within your purview, I must ask you to make an exception. Mrs. Vogel's nephew, Mr. Steven Rutledge, has deserted his post in Manchester. He was last seen heading towards Derbyshire and is believed to be concealed in Leicester. Once you have apprehended him, return him to his commanding officer in Manchester.*

*Please have the utmost care of discretion in this matter as Mrs. Vogels family would like to avoid a scandal. I assured her that I trust no one's discretion so much as I trust yours.*

*General Vogel*

Richard looked at the clock upon the mantel and assessed the time. It was late, but if he left now he would have a better chance of apprehending the deserter before word got out that he had been traced. Deserters assume someone will be sent after them, and rarely do they stay in one place long. Luck had been with Richard in the past when he had performed these sort of personal favors for his commanding officer. He prayed this time would be no different and that it would take remarkably little effort on his part to apprehend the man. The only delay he could foresee was location. The other favors had been carried out it London, where Richard had resources and connections that he did not have here in the wild and untamed wilderness of the north. He was unsure how long this job would take him.

Richard called for his horse to be readied, packed some clothing in his satchel, and penned a short note to Anne.

*Dearest Anne,*

*My General has called me away on business that cannot be delayed. I do not know when I shall return.*

*I have thought more about our conversation tonight and am convinced you should marry another. As you can see, I am wedded to the life of the army and am often called off at a moment's notice. I love the life I live and am not ready to give it up for the life of a gentleman. It would not be fair to ask you to leave your ancestral home to follow my nomadic lifestyle, so I beg of you, please go to London and find another to love.*

*Richard*

Richard walked to Anne's room and listened for a moment before slipping the note under the door. He could hear movement in the room and an occasional cough or sniffle, no doubt brought on by her tears. He could listen no longer. He left Pemberley under the black sky of the cold December night.

# Chapter 17

The day of the Bennets' departure soon came, and Mrs. Bennet was forced to submit to a separation which seemed all the worse because her dear Jane had announced her eminent relocation to the north. Their departure was far more vocal than when the Darcys had left Longbourn the day of their wedding, for she did not have the enjoyment of the day's events to distract her.

"Oh! My dear Lizzy," she cried, "when will we meet again?"

"Soon, Mamma. Fitzwilliam has promised me we will visit Hertfordshire often."

"What an agreeable man he is; so thoughtful of your happiness. You are exceedingly blessed, Lizzy. Write to me very often, my dear. I must know how you are doing. Remember, I would be happy to offer you advice any time you should ask. I have rarely had such a pleasant time as we did speaking last night."

"Thank you, Mamma. I will write as often as I can."

"Jane, come here, dear. I need a hug." Mrs. Bennet held open her arms until Jane walked into them. Embracing her tightly, Mrs. Bennet prattled, "Now, you make sure Mr. Bingley's carriage is warm enough. I would not want you to catch a chill on your way home. When you return, I will come and visit you." Jane looked at Charles with wide eyes. He shrugged his shoulders in a defeated action. Both were glad that soon they would move to their new situation.

Fitzwilliam's adieus were heartfelt and sincere. Never had he imagined he would come to love his wife's family as he had, despite the turmoil and contention that had been caused by them. He advised Mrs. Lacroix to have a basket of food prepared for their journey home, and he had extra pillows, warming stones, and rugs added to their carriage. He had thought of everything to make their trip more pleasant.

Georgiana, Mary, and Kitty cried. They were distressed that they knew not when they would see one another again. Even a promise from Fitzwilliam that Georgiana could go with them on their next trip to Hertfordshire did not satisfy, for they had not yet set a date. The girls promised to write regularly, and soon Fitzwilliam was considering the economy of hiring his own man to carry letters between Pemberley and Longbourn, for there were bound to be many.

Once the Bennet carriage pulled from the drive, Elizabeth and Jane stood at the drawing room window watching it clatter down the road until it was no longer visible. Fitzwilliam and Charles both knew their wives already missed their parents and younger sisters, though they tried not to show it.

Soon after, their attention was drawn to a commotion on the staircase.

"Uncle! Uncle!" Anne shouted in a frenzy. "Oh! Where is my uncle?"

Elizabeth stepped from the drawing room just in time to hear Fitzwilliam address her. "I do not think he has come down yet this morning. What is the matter?"

Anne waved a piece of paper towards him, which he took from her. Turning it over, he began to read as Anne provided Elizabeth with a summary. "It is Richard. He has left on army business. That is not all of it, either. He has broken our engagement. The worst part about it is he penned it in a letter. The least he could have done was had the decency to wake me and tell me in person." Anne paced back and forth in front of them. "The presumption of Richard to think I would allow him to break our engagement so easily. No! I will not have it. I know he loves me, and I love him. He says he agrees with my mother that I should marry a wealthy man who can save Rosings Park. I will not have it. My mother shall not triumph and ruin my chance for happiness."

Elizabeth tried to calm Anne and get her to stop rambling, but she would not. Anne had worked herself into a frenzy, and nothing but Richard returning to Pemberley would put her at ease.

"Of course I shall triumph. I always do," Lady Catherine cooed from the top of the stairs. She had overheard her daughter and was pleased with the situation. "Richard has more sense than I gave him credit for. I am mightily proud of him for understanding the situation and taking matters into his own hands."

"I hate you, Mother!" Anne said through clenched teeth, and then turned towards her uncle's room.

It was a full hour before Fitzwilliam, Lord Matlock, and James located the stable boy who had saddled Richard's horse late last night. The boy knew little, just that Richard had called for his horse to be saddled, and that he had left in his uniform with a full set of saddlebags. He had not given the boy any indication of when he would return, nor did he say where he was going.

The entire party was left to await his return and console a distraught Anne.

## Chapter 18

The departure of the Bennets the day before had been the beginning of the Pemberley guests returning to their homes after the holiday. Today James and Roslynd were leaving with their three adorable children.

Elizabeth was sad to see them go, for she had thoroughly enjoyed having the children's laughter brighten the rooms of the manor.

With the distressing matters of the financial affairs of Rosings Park and the possible wedding of Anne and Richard being unresolved, Lord and Lady Matlock felt it prudent to extend their stay. James and Evelyn were upset they would not be able to ride home in their grandparents carriage. They begged and pleaded, citing how well they had behaved, but it did no good. They must leave today, and it was yet undetermined when the others would return.

Lady Matlock offered them hugs and promises that they could come stay with her as soon as she returned to Matlock, and, at long last, they entered their father's carriage wiping the tears from their eyes.

The manor was slowly becoming a quieter place as more and more of the family left.

A full week had passed since Richard's departure. Anne could hardly maintain a rationality about her. The longer he was away, the more she despaired of his returning for her. Lord Matlock insisted she meet with him and Fitzwilliam each morning to be tutored in estate business. They were determined she would possess at least a basic understanding of all estate matters before leaving Pemberley. They were determined that, upon her return to Rosings Park, she would be able to make sound decisions regarding its improvement. Mr. Johnson could not be more pleased with Anne's ability to understand all the men taught her. He was confident that upon her return to Rosings Park the two of them could restore the estate to its previous state of grandeur.

By the middle of the first week of January, Lady Catherine's restlessness had become unbearable, and she demanded she be allowed to return to Rosings Park. The last thing any of them wanted was for her to return unaccompanied; there was no telling what she would do.

Anne understood they could not remain at Pemberley forever, and already she was eager to return to her own home now that she understood its fate. She was determined to begin setting the estate affairs in order and stop its continued failure.

Her fear was she would leave Pemberley only to have Richard return here for her. Anne had sent letters to every known lodging Richard frequented in hopes he would receive one and know she expected him to come for her at Rosings Park. It was time for her to go home.

Lady Matlock accompanied Anne back to Rosings Park. Their conversation was in abundance. Anne wanted to learn everything she could about the man she loved, and likewise Lady Matlock thought it best to get to know her future daughter-in-law, for she was sure there would still be a wedding. Though the two women were related, the distance between their homes and the short visits of their past had not provided them ample opportunity to know one another as well as they ought.

The conversation in the second carriage, however, was stilted. Mile after mile passed in silence between Lord Matlock and his sister. The closer they came to Rosings Park, the more indignant she became. Lady Catherine had already been informed by Anne that she would have two days to gather her belongings and move to the Dower House. Lady Matlock had been asked to keep an eye on Lady Catherine, No one trusted her simply to pack her belongings and leave the place; they all feared she would cause more damage to Rosings Park.

The third carriage conveyed the Darcys. It had not been their intent to leave Pemberley this winter, but under the present circumstances Fitzwilliam felt a sort of responsibility to Anne. He had not taken lightly the charge from his aunt to review the Rosings Park ledgers, and he was appalled that he did not notice her duplicity. The fact that his aunt had pulled the wool over his eyes angered him beyond reason. Fitzwilliam planned to assist his uncle and Anne in any way he could. Elizabeth cared not where they travelled, even if the destination was Rosings Park, so long as they were together.

Georgiana remained behind with the Bingleys, who had been invited to stay at Pemberley as long as they wanted. Their continued presence would provide company for Georgiana until her companion returned the following week. As an added bonus, it would offer the newly married couple the privacy they had been missing in at Netherfield. They were happy to accept the invitation, and took the opportunity to drive to their newly let estate where Jane took measurements for her new curtains and spoke to Charles about how she would like the furniture placed. Both of them were counting the days until they could take up residence there, sure that it would offer them every bit of happiness they dreamed of.

Richard had been in Leicester for ten days. He already knew where the deserter was. He had seen him twice the first day he had arrived, but twice he had not arrested him.

He had continued to see the man each day thereafter, but still he did not arrest him. Something held him back.

When he had left Pemberley he had been sure breaking his engagement with Anne was the right thing to do. In the beginning, he continually repeated in his mind it was the best thing for her, though his heart refused to listen. But the more days that had passed, the more miserable Richard became and the less sure he was.

In previous assignments, he had easily apprehended deserters, returned them to their commanding officers, filed the requisite paperwork, and returned to his lifestyle of leisure, all within three days' time. Not this time. His heart just was not in it. Once he arrested the deserter and returned him, what then? Would he return to Pemberley? London? His lack of resolve with regards to his own life made it nearly impossible for him to complete his assignment.

Finally, he could wait no longer. If he did not apprehend the man and take him in, then General Vogel would send another. In any case, he was tired of sleeping in a bed that was not his own and wearing the same clothing day in and day out. If nothing else, apprehending the man would allow him to return to civilized society, even if he was miserable and discontent with his life in general.

When he made the decision to arrest Mr. Rutledge, carrying it out was easy. With as many times as the colonel had seen him, he had also been seen. The man had at first suspected the colonel was there to apprehend him, but as the days passed and the colonel had never made his move, the man had relaxed and let down his guard.

Colonel Fitzwilliam escorted Mr. Rutledge's transport to Manchester, where he handed him over to his commanding officer and then went to the local office to file the required paperwork.

"Good God, man, what took you so long?" the militia secretary squawked as Colonel Fitzwilliam entered and sat down at a vacant desk across from the man who had been his friend for many years.

Colonel Fitzwilliam grumbled something incoherent and picked up a pen, dipping it in ink.

"What is the matter? You are not acting like yourself, man. What has gotten into you?"

"Nothing!"

"Ah, I see. You have been slighted by a woman."

"I have not been slighted," Colonel Fitzwilliam barked back, but then he breathed out a sigh of resignation. "I was the one doing the slighting, and I wholeheartedly regret it. Would you believe that ten days ago I was engaged?"

"Engaged? Not you!"

"Yes, it is true, but alas, I was a fool and broke it off."

"Why?" his friend questioned.

"Because, as I said, I am a fool, that is why."

"Well, at least the ladies of London will not have to experience the pain of broken hearts because the infamous Colonel Fitzwilliam is off the marriage market," he retorted.

"Do not be callous, man. I am in serious pain here."

"I am not being callous. I have heard the ladies speak of you often. The day you publically announce your engagement, the streets of London will be flooded by the tears of wailing women."

"Fear not, for that day will never come.

I have lost my only true love. I shall never marry another."

"She must be some woman to have you pining away over her as you are."

"She is."

No more was said between the two until Colonel Fitzwilliam handed the man his paperwork and rose to leave. "Colonel Fitzwilliam, I sincerely hope you find happiness. If you love this woman as you say you do, I think you should return and tell her. She may be pining away for you as you are for her." He looked at Colonel Fitzwilliam who said not a word. "It is worth a chance, is it not?"

Colonel Fitzwilliam nodded and left the room. His mind raced with possibilities. He had loved Anne for years, but he had never let his mind linger on her because he thought there was no chance of their marriage. Now, he had tasted the sweetness of her kisses, held her soft body against his, and he knew there was only one thing left to do. He must marry her. He would return to Pemberley immediately and ask for her forgiveness, even beg if he needed to.

The return ride to Pemberley seemed longer than it ever had before. The anticipation of seeing Anne made each mile pass more slowly than usual. Richard's thoughts ran through hundreds of scenarios of what he would say to Anne, but in the end none of them felt right. He wished he could tell her what was in his heart, but military men were not supposed to be sensitive, and all of his training told him to use logic. In the end, as Pemberley came into view, his heart won out. He was determined to seek out Anne and tell her just how much he loved her.

The Pemberley butler opened the front door with precision timing as Richard reached the top step. Georgiana had been informed of his riding up the drive and was there with the Bingleys to greet him.

"Richard, you are back! We did not expect you," Georgiana said as she reached out and wrapped him in a hug.

"You did not? Why not? I said I would return."

"I just assumed you would have received word that everyone left for Rosings Park, and joined them there."

Richard's face fell at the news. "Anne is not here?"

"No, she is not, and you should be ashamed of yourself," Georgiana scolded.

"Had you been here, Miss de Bourgh very well may have taken your head off," Charles jested. "You put that woman through more misery than you can imagine."

"She was upset, then?"

"Upset? Harrumph! That is an understatement. Not only did she have to deal with the distress of a broken engagement, but then she had to listen to her gloating mother. I think you will have some serious explaining to do when you return to her," said Charles.

"She is very angry then?"

"Not angry, per se," Jane chimed in with all her sweetness, "but all of her hopes of happiness have been shattered."

"If it were me, I would not want to see you again unless you had changed your mind," said Georgiana.

"I have, Georgie, I have!" Richard spoke quickly, trying to emphasize how he had changed. "I rode back here as fast as I could with the intent to tell Anne how much I love her."

"Then you had better get cleaned up, have something to eat, rest well tonight, and then make haste to Rosings Park. It is likely to take you four days complete to get there in this weather. I will make sure a carriage is ready for you in the morning."

"No, Georgie, I will go on horseback."

"On horseback! Richard, it is too far to go on horseback in this weather. You should use the carriage. I assure you, we will not miss it. It is safer this way."

"I can travel much faster on horseback. It is likely I can take off a full day, perhaps two, from my journey if I ride."

"Very well, but if you get sick with pneumonia, do not say I did not warn you."

## Chapter 19

Richard was an hour into his journey before the pink hue of the January sunrise blazed across the horizon to the east of him. Already his fingers and toes were numb, but he did not regret his decision to ride. The two hundred miles between Pemberley and Rosings Park could more speedily be covered on horseback. He stopped for a late breakfast in Leicester at the inn where he had recently spent ten days. He was well pleased at the pace he had set. The fifty miles from Pemberley to Leicester was normally a half-day journey in a carriage on good roads. He calculated the distance, determined to get as far as Luton for the night. If he could make it that far, the remaining seventy-five miles would be an easy trip tomorrow.

He was determined to reach his destination, and when he fell exhausted into his bed at the Luton Inn that night he praised his good fortune. The farther south he travelled, the warmer the weather became, and the roads more passable. He was certain he would make it to Rosings Park in a reasonable time tomorrow.

The following morning Richard was on his way south again. During his ride the previous day he had made many decisions and had resolved to stop in London to meet with his commanding officer.

Tapping on the general's office door, he heard him command, "Enter!"

"Sir—"

"Colonel Fitzwilliam, I did not expect you back in London until the end of the month. Thank you for your assistance in that delicate matter."

"You are welcome, sir."

"Very good. Well, what can I do for you?"

Richard took a long, drawn-out breath. Once he made his request, there would be no going back. "Sir, I have had the happy fortune of meeting lady—"

"Congratulations! Do I know her?" The general had long been a married man and highly approved of all his officers having wives. A woman calmed even the most wild man and gave him a sense of responsibility.

"No, sir, I do not believe you do, though you may have heard of her family; the de Bourgh's of Rosings Park in Kent."

"de Bourgh ... de Bourgh ... No, I do not believe I know them."

"Yes, well, that is not the part I came here to discuss. Miss de Bourgh is the heiress to Rosings Park, and when we marry I will be taking up the responsibilities of master of her estate."

General Vogel was beginning to understand what the colonel had come to discuss. "Ah, I see. You wish to sell your commission."

"Yes, sir, I do. Today I want only to notify you of my intent, but I will return before the end of the month to file the necessary paperwork."

"When is the wedding?"

Richard assessed his general, and then resolved to tell him the absolute truth. "Sir, may I be frank?"

"Of course," General Vogel said, eyeing Colonel Fitzwilliam suspiciously.

"Miss de Bourgh is my cousin. We have known one another since infancy. The past ten years complete we have loved one another, but we have never been able to declare ourselves because of family politics. You know how it is." The general nodded and gestured for the colonel to continue. "This Christmas we were able to come to an understanding, but a few days later we found out her mother has run her rather large and once profitable estate to ruin. All of Miss de Bourgh's inheritance, except her dowry, is gone, and she is forced with the possibility of losing her estate. Though her dowry is a rather large one, I felt it prudent to break our engagement to allow her the opportunity to find a wealthier man, one who could bring a fortune to their marriage and help her restore her home. However, I have since determined I was wrong. I simply cannot allow the woman I love to marry another. I am on my way to Kent to reunite with her, beg her forgiveness, and see if she will take me back."

"Well, that is quite a story you have there. I thought sagas such as this only took place in those books my wife likes to read." He laughed heartily and leaned forward in his chair. "Do you think she will take you back?"

"I certainly hope so."

"What will you do if she does not?"

Richard's shoulders sagged as he slowly replied, "Work by her side to help her restore her home, begging her forgiveness night and day until she relents."

"So, you are determined to give up your commission even if she will not immediately take you back?"

"I am."

"Very well, I will make some inquiries and have the papers ready when you return. Send me word a few days before you arrive."

"Thank you, sir."

"Is that everything?" said General Vogel.

"Yes, sir, it is."

"You are dismissed."

Richard nodded and turned to leave the room. He paused when General Vogel addressed him as his hand reached for the door. "Colonel Fitzwilliam, I will be sad to see you leave the army, but I approve of your decision. I always say a man needs the love of a good woman. I hope your Miss de Bourgh will be a loving wife for you."

"Thank you, sir. There is no one else I could ever imagine being with."

Richard was in high spirits when he rode the remaining forty miles to Kent. He had a plan, and every good soldier knew that the way to win a war was to have a clear plan.

It was nearing three o'clock in the afternoon when Richard espied the chimneys of Rosings Park peeking through the trees. He urged his horse on, both eager and apprehensive to see Anne again.

When the stable boy took his horse, Richard threw his saddlebags over his shoulder and walked up the front stairs. Ringing the bell, he heard a commotion on the other side, but no one came to the door. Richard stood a moment, waiting, until finally he gave up and opened the door himself. He stepped inside to find his parents and Anne arguing with Lady Catherine. The Darcys were standing off to the side, trying to keep out of the fray. No one noticed him at first, and he soon gathered the reason for the argument; Anne was adamant her mother should leave the manor and move into the Dower House.

"Mother, you should have left days ago. I have been lenient until now, but I will not allow you to question my authority or advise the servants in opposition of my desires."

"No, Anne, I will not. I have far too many memories here, and I refuse to leave." Lady Catherine sat down in the chair near the door, determined to stay put. It was clear to Richard that her stubbornness was acting in her favor, and unless his parents and Anne changed their methods the outcome was inevitable. Richard made his presence known when he reigned in his aunt and turned the tides of the battle in their favor. He had the element of surprise, which was highly in his favor as he commanded their attention. "Aunt, you will desist your offensive behaviour and act as a guest should, for that is what you are: a guest at Rosings Park."

"Richard!" said Anne, when she saw him. She hurried to where he stood and threw her arms around him. Not a word was said; she simply commanded a kiss from him, in front of the entire party.

Lord Matlock cleared his throat to garner their attention, but then he had to grab his side in pain as his wife elbowed him.

"You have come to me. I am so glad."

"Oh, Anne, I have much to tell you! But first we must settle the problem of your mother." Richard kissed her forehead gently and then returned his attention to his aunt. Taking Lady Catherine by the elbow, he pulled her to her feet and led her to the door. Then, calling to the footman to follow him with her trunks, he escorted her all the way to the estate's Dower House.

Anne paced the foyer, counting each second he was away from her. The past fortnight had been the hardest she had ever endured. The fear of losing her ancestral home was nothing to the heartbreak she had been experiencing by having Richard break their engagement and leave her alone.

She had been at Rosings Park for little more than a week, but already she, her uncle, Fitzwilliam, and Mr. Johnson had made ample progress towards ceasing the financial drains on the estate. They were close to knowing the full extent of the deficit and would then be able to determine what would be needed to restore the estate to its previous state of profitability. Anne prayed it would not be more than her dowry. Her mind was somewhat eased when her uncle told her that no matter the cost, he would ensure she did not lose Rosings Park.

When the door opened and admitted Richard for a second time that afternoon,

Anne stopped her pacing and looked at him. She feared her eyes were deceiving her, that he was not actually there, until his strong arms circled her and drew her close.

"Anne, I am a fool. Can you ever forgive me?"

Anne looked into his eyes, willing to forgive him anything if he would promise to stay with her. Her heart was too overcome to let her speak, but she nodded.

"How could I ever believe I could live without you? The past two weeks have been torturous for me. My heart longed to be with you, but my head told me I should not be so selfish. I reasoned that you needed a man with fortune, but then in the very next moment my heart would take over again, and I knew that so long as we are together everything will work out. I know if we work together we can restore Rosings Park. It may take every penny we have, and every ounce of our energy, but I know we can do it together." Pausing, he looked into her eyes, which had misted over with tears of happiness. "Anne, I must tell you how much I love you. I love you with every ounce of my soul. Will you marry me?"

"Yes, Richard, nothing could make me happier."

The two shared a passionate embrace that Richard pulled out of first. "I have more to tell you."

"More? What else can you possibly have to say that cannot wait until later? I would prefer another kiss."

"As tempting as that is, I must tell you everything. On my way here, I stopped in London and told my general that I want to sell my commission. It is my intention to help you restore your home and make it my own."

Though it was not what she expected, nothing he could have said would have made Anne happier. She raised up on her tiptoes and commanded another kiss from him. His tender kisses were a balm to her troubled soul. With him, everything was possible.

# Chapter 20

Although Anne had always considered him handsome in his uniform, when she entered the chapel on the arm of her uncle and saw Richard standing at the front in his grey coat, she thought he had never been so handsome. She could hardly believe she was finally marrying her true love, and rejoiced that she and Richard would never be parted again.

Anne had been relieved when Richard returned and confessed he could not live without her, that he had chosen to sell his commission and become the master of Rosings Park so long as she would have him. No woman had ever agreed as fast as she had, nor planned an entire wedding so quickly.

Anne cared not for the large fanfare of a London wedding. No, she wanted a simple wedding at the Hunsford Chapel, as soon as possible.

Anne Fitzwilliam nee de Bourgh was one of the happiest brides Elizabeth Darcy had ever laid eyes upon. Her entire being glowed with warmth and happiness whenever she looked upon her new husband. It was a look Elizabeth knew well, for after two full months of being married she still looked upon her husband in the same way.

The Darcys left Kent not long after Richard and Anne's wedding. Their return trip would take three days, but happily for them the weather was mild and the roads well maintained. Elizabeth reclined in the seat against Fitzwilliam, his arms wrapped tightly around her as she rested her head against his chest, a rug placed across their laps for warmth.

"Fitzwilliam," Elizabeth said, "though our first Christmas was much more exciting than we thought it would be, I think it turned out well."

"I agree," Fitzwilliam responded, kissing the top of Elizabeth's head.

Elizabeth tilted her head to look into his eyes. Smiling, she asked, "Do you think we will ever be able to top it?"

Fitzwilliam laughed, strengthening his hold around Elizabeth. "I certainly hope not. I prefer that our next Christmas be fraught with dullness."

"Oh no, I would never want that. I love the pomp and fanfare of a festive season." Elizabeth continued to hold the gaze of her loving husband. "Oh, I have the perfect solution!" she exclaimed.

"And what would that be?" Fitzwilliam asked curiously.

"I think we should fill the house with children and enjoy an intimate family party."

A broad smile spread across Fitzwilliam's face as he responded, "What a perfect idea." Then, tipping his head towards his beautiful wife, he kissed her in such a manner there was no question that he agreed with her proposal.

# Epilogue

With the Darcys, Richard and Anne were always on the most intimate terms; they really loved them and they were both ever sensible of the warmest gratitude towards the persons who had supported their love match from the beginning.

I wish I could say, for the sake of the couple, that their happiness was all that was needed to make Lady Catherine de Bourgh sanction their marriage, but it was not. Lady Catherine was extremely indignant on the marriage of her daughter and nephew, and as she gave way to all the genuine frankness of her character, she announced that she would not sanction the marriage and would not allow Anne or her husband in her presence ever again. Lady Catherine lived the remainder of her days isolated at the Dower House, and in the end she died bitter and alone, not once setting eyes upon her grandchildren who Lord and Lady Matlock loved so much. Lord and Lady Matlock were determined that Richard should be successful as the master of Rosings Park; their affection for their son and new daughter-in-law drew them oftener from home to Rosings Park, and they delighted in arriving especially when they were least expected.

Lady Catherine had indeed run the estate into financial ruin, but luckily it was not so far gone that it could not be recovered with the resources Anne and Richard had available between her dowry and the sale of his commission. To further the restoration efforts, Lord Matlock met with his eldest son, and the two of them agreed to settle Richard's inheritance upon him immediately rather than wait for the Earl's death.

It seemed like a long time, but in actuality it was only three years before Anne and her husband returned the estate to its previous state of grandeur. Under Richard's care the estate thrived, and in another five years complete it matched the profitability of Pemberley.

*The End*

# About EMMALINE

"From an early age I have always been fascinated by the written word and the mood and atmosphere it creates for a reader; especially those books that affect me and transport me to some far-off place. These are the elements I strive to create in my books. My books in many ways record what most affects me: my feelings and experiences with family, friends, and those I have run into on my life's journey. My hope is that in my books you will find something that touches you, something which will resonate in your soul and remind you that you are strong and can overcome anything, especially if you have the support of loving friends and family." - Emmaline Hoffmeister

Emmaline Hoffmeister was born and raised in the Pacific Northwest, but spent 9 years traveling as much as possible with her husband and two sons so she didn't have to deal with the cold. In 2020, she returned to the Wenatchee Valley in Central Washington where she now tolerates the frigidly cold winters by curling up in front of the fire with her laptop and soft yellow blanket. When writer's block sets in she stares at the rainbows covering her walls from the crystals hanging in her windows.

Emmaline is the wife of her very own Mr. Darcy and mother to two amazing sons. Emmaline centers her life around her family and her faith which brings her joy each and every day of her life.

You can find all of Emmaline Hoffmeister's other published novels at her website www.emmalinehoffmeister.com.

Emmaline loves to hear from readers, feel free to email her at emmalinehoffmeister@gmail.com.

Printed in Great Britain
by Amazon